'*Fortune* careens across history's epochs in the same way it gallops from continent to continent, its characters traversing a stage from Napoleonic Prussia to South America and Van Diemen's Land. It's an audacious, brilliantly crafted take on history—a novel about the past like no other. It draws your breath in the same way as if you'd witnessed a jigsaw puzzle tossed and scattered into the air only to have its pieces land on the ground in perfect unity.'—Paul Daley, *Guardian Australia*

'*Fortune* is a supremely entertaining novel—witty, gripping and endlessly surprising—told with energy and charm. Lenny's great talent is showing that even if the upheavals of history are usually set in motion by famous individuals, it is those lost to history who are left to pick up the pieces and find their way through the ensuing chaos.'—Chris Womersley, author of *Bereft* and *City of Crows*

'A thrilling tale of adventure told across centuries and continents . . . It made me laugh and cry and swear with astonishment. It is savage and nihilistic, wise and kind, never less than gripping, and it is over far sooner than you want it to be. And every line is marked with the author's unmistakable stylistic signature: somewhere between Roger Federer at the net and Mick Jagger's rooster strut.'—Geordie Williamson, Chief Literary Critic, *The Australian*

PRAISE FOR *INFAMY*

'Bartulin has written a truly exciting book, a nightmare tale of pursuit glimpsed in vivid fragments. He has revealed a capacious talent, assured even as it seems reckless.' —Peter Pierce, *The Weekend Australian*

'*Infamy* is a novel that satisfies on every level. Intensely cinematic—imagine Martin Scorsese let loose in Van Diemen's Land—it distils the colonial experience down to its elemental violence. With vivid characters, deep psychological understanding and symphonic plotting, it drew me in so completely that it was a shock to find out that this is a work of the imagination. Bartulin has made fiction stranger, and more compelling, than truth. A Tassie devil of a book.'—Malcolm Knox

'A rip-snorting, swashbuckling Aussie western set in the early part of the nation's history . . . Bartulin gives a visceral sense of the place, of the heat and isolation that bubbles up through savage drinking binges and dockland murders, whorehouses and massacres. *Infamy* is an excellent read. It is a book that gets the blood flowing and the fist pounding, and makes you glad you don't live by a dockyard tavern in 1830s Tasmania.'—*Sydney Morning Herald*

'All the requisite ingredients for a retro, rollicking tale are duly assembled. A great Tasmanian rogue, Errol Flynn, would have relished bringing the role of Burr to the screen . . . Tasmania deserves an encore from Bartulin.'—*Canberra Times*

'This Australian Western draws on Tasmania's early penal history and results in a highly original concept and storyline, which will keep you intrigued until the final page.'—*Sunday Tasmanian*

'A rollicking, dark tale set in the bloody midst of Tasmania's colonial past.'—*Books+Publishing*

'*Infamy* is a superbly rendered piece of historical fiction, a dark, almost noir crime story, and a unique and unashamedly Australian take on the western.'—*The King's Tribune*

'Outrageous, fast-paced and exhilarating . . . it's Errol Flynn meets Tarantino in a *Deadwood* down-under. Lenny Bartulin has an exciting new voice in historical adventure that goes well beyond old-fashioned swash-and-buckle and confidently busts loose into new territory. Brilliant!' —The Historical Novel Society

'A panoramic vision of the madness and mayhem of Australia's early colonial experience and a highly enjoyable raucous adventure.'—Readings

Lenny Bartulin's previous novel, *Infamy*, was longlisted in the 2015 Tasmanian Premier's Literary Awards. He has lived in Sydney, the Blue Mountains and currently resides in Hobart with his wife and son.

FORTUNE

Lenny Bartulin

ALLEN&UNWIN
SYDNEY・MELBOURNE・AUCKLAND・LONDON

p. 292: Stendhal, Article 8, *Les Privilèges*, translation by Simon Leys, reproduced from Simon Leys, *With Stendhal*, Black Inc., 2010

   This project has been assisted by the Australian Government through the Australia Council, its arts funding and advisory board.

 This project was assisted through Arts Tasmania by the Minister for the Arts.

Allen & Unwin
83 Alexander Street
Crows Nest NSW 2065
Australia
Phone: (61 2) 8425 0100
Email: info@allenandunwin.com
Web: www.allenandunwin.com

 A catalogue record for this book is available from the National Library of Australia

ISBN 978 1 76052 930 7

Set in 13.5/18.2 pt Bodoni LT Pro by Bookhouse, Sydney
Printed and bound in Australia by Griffin Press, part of Ovato

10 9 8 7 6 5 4 3 2 1

For Luka,
boy wonder

. . . but the gods who live beneath
names and above places have gone
off without a word and outsiders
have settled in their place.

Italo Calvino, *Invisible Cities*

BOOK I

ALWAYS BEGIN WITH THE FACTS

The little man was riding a beautiful white horse, they say, the day he marched into Berlin. Of course he was. Who'd sit Napoleon on a mule?

But, really, it doesn't matter. Time sullies every truth. History can't tell you a thing for sure. Well, maybe the date.

It was 27 October 1806.

L'ENTRÉE DE NAPOLÉON À BERLIN

Johannes Meyer was there, in the crowd gathered along Unter den Linden, as cool late-afternoon shadows fell from the buildings and the victorious Grande Armée followed their emperor through the Brandenburg Gate. He was a young man of eighteen years and no particular talent, was like other young men of his generation, those who tended towards romantic poetry, aimless walks in the woods, passionate ideals debated until dawn in the smoky din of coffee houses. Their heroes were Goethe and Schiller and Humboldt, and they could recite passages by heart. They had no money and the future was a bright dream of unbounded freedom and promise. Their mothers worried and their fathers thought them useless.

Johannes Meyer had no parents to contend with, but no matter how hard he pushed, he simply couldn't get through the crowd to catch even a glimpse of Napoleon Bonaparte.

'Hey, leave off!' the man in front of him said and thrust back with his elbow, catching the boy in the ribs. 'Want me to knuckle you, son?'

His friends were all gone, they'd managed to slip through, but Johannes remained caught at the rear, a lonely leaf in the swirling current.

EVERYTHING HAPPENS, ALL THE TIME

The crowd was vast. They'd come to see the most famous man on earth, the most feared, the most powerful, the man who'd just crushed mighty Prussia at the battles of Jena and Auerstedt, each a mere afternoon's work. The man who'd sacked the kings and bishops, the man who'd made the Creole an empress. Often, people were disappointed seeing him up close (Bonaparte could always tell and it made him cranky and cruel) but on a white horse at the head of his men, triumphant, surrounded by his preening maréchals and généraux, all jostling their mounts to be nearer, eager for reflected glory, the Emperor was all that could be imagined, and more.

The Prussian crowd was silent, the men awed, the women in turmoil. The women endured the grip of an unpatriotic lust.

Many succumbed, the energy around them was too intense, impossible to resist. All those lonely soldiers' wives, the widows, the daughters. And from the most wretched, toothless canonniers, to the eau de cologne colonels, the French reaped desire that day and for a score of days to come, thanks to their short, magnificent leader.

'*Vive l'Empereur!*'

Johannes Meyer, too.

Her name was Beatrice Reiss and she'd recognised him instantly; he was tall and looked lost as always, that face, a blush of boyish softness on the cusp of rugged manhood. Dark curly hair, and the dimple in his cheek when he smiled. He often came to the coffee house where she served, arriving with his handsome young friends, laughing and embracing one another, drinking and arguing into the early morning. She'd seen him in the crowd just now and squeezed through the endless shoulders, forced her way over, and then she was standing right beside him, their arms touching, pressed full length. Without a word, without even thinking to do it, she took Johannes Meyer by the hand.

He felt the grip, the moist heat of her palm, and turned to look, his face a question.

Beatrice smiled. The girl from the coffee house.

Her hair was red and plaited down the back, with curling wisps escaping over small ears that stuck out from her head. Pale and freckled, pink-lipped and wide-mouthed, Beatrice wasn't much older than Johannes but knew far more. This deeper mystery was there in her hazel eyes; the boy saw it and was unable to resist. He'd thought of her often enough, back in his cold attic room, and now here she was.

Beatrice pulled him down towards her, said into his ear, 'Come with me.'

Johannes followed as she led him out from the crowd. They held hands and turned left and right and then left again, at first against the endless stream of people, soon into less congested streets. Further on, in a clean, wide cobbled lane, Beatrice found a door and opened it with a key, rushed them both in. She called out once and confirmed nobody was there, then fell upon a couch and pulled up her skirts. She motioned to the boy, his face still asking something of her, and embarrassed now, too.

'Johannes,' she said.

He hesitated: a childish fear.

She repeated his name, but softer, breathless. She held out her arms.

He went to her on the couch.

Everything happens, all the time. It had just never happened to Johannes Meyer before.

PISTOLS

Nothing much had ever happened to Stendhal either, apart from syphilis.

He was also in Berlin that day, in the crowd at the Brandenburg Gate, though his name was still Marie-Henri Beyle and nobody had ever heard of him. Twenty-three and plump, with a wispy jawline beard and fancy hair, fired by grand artistic ambitions all currently on hold as he endured the duties of an adjutant military commissary (family connections). Under his coat were two loaded pistols. Wary of the crush of people, he'd held his elbows pressed in, hands up at his chest, and walked in a strange, stiff manner all day. He mentioned the pistols when he wrote his sister later that night, but of course said nothing about posing in front of the mirror in his room, arm extended and taking aim side-on, head high and saying to his reflection, 'Sir, you have injured my good name. Prepare thyself . . .' and other versions of the same, though he was unable, in the end, to settle upon a final wording.

In the same letter to his sister, Henri Beyle wrote of the Emperor: *For the entrance, Napoleon wore the dress uniform of a* général *de division. It is perhaps the only time I ever saw him. He was riding about twenty paces in front of the soldiers; the silent crowd stood only about two paces from his horse. Anybody could have fired a gun at him, from any one of the windows.*

Further on, he added: *I don't know what gave them the idea to put a city in the middle of all this sand.*

Like the posing with the pistols in his room, young Henri didn't mention seeing Johannes and Beatrice through the window either.

After leaving the crowd on Unter den Linden and heading back to his billet, he'd heard the unmistakable sounds of human passion. The future Stendhal stopped before the window, shocked, and listened intently to the soft, rhythmic groans of pleasure. He checked the street, up and down, then pressed his face to the window glass and cupped his hands around his eyes.

He watched and watched, until he heard footsteps at the corner. He continued watching even as they approached and grew louder, holding his breath, unwilling to relinquish the sight. Finally, at the last moment, he swore and dashed away, delighted and thrilled, a memory of Berlin he'd never forget.

More of him later.

FIRST SIGHT

Elisabeth von Hoffmann came around the corner and noticed a man running away down the lane. He looked funny, unnatural, elbows clamped tight at his sides, like little wings pinned to his coat.

She was with her aunt's secretary, Günther Jagelman, who was old and deaf and so didn't hear the breathless sounds of lovemaking through the window as they passed. But Elisabeth von Hoffmann heard, and she turned in her stride and saw, disbelieving, the couple on the couch. She forgot about the running man and his chicken wings. All the downy blonde hairs on her arms and scalp lifted, and she felt something like a surge of cold well-water from her head to her toes.

Elisabeth was seventeen years old and locked inside the heated tumult of a young body. Her skin was sensitive to even the thought of a touch; her nights were long and sleepless in her transforming. She was overwhelmed by love and longing, could hardly wait to enter the world and be found by this love, a dream of such exquisite possibility that it seemed inevitable. Instead, she found herself in a constant state of anticipation, disappointment and, ultimately, boredom.

It was torture. It was all she could do to endure another day at her aunt's home, endure another day in Berlin, caught inside her life like a bird in a cage. With the news of Bonaparte's victories and impending arrival in the city, she'd felt neither fear nor loss but, rather, hope; this was the glorious upheaval she'd been praying for. There is no greater freedom than things being taken out of our hands.

The messengers had come and gone all morning with news of Bonaparte's progress towards the capital until at last, unbelievably, he was there. Aunt Margaretha had forbidden it at first, but Elisabeth had convinced Günther to take her, and so they'd gone together to see the Corsican ogre. The crowd, unfortunately, was enormous and impossible to penetrate; they'd arrived too late. Like Johannes Meyer, they left without even a glimpse.

Behind them now, Elisabeth felt the silence and the hush that pressed down on the crowd when Napoleon appeared in their midst. And it was just then that she heard the strains of passion, too, and looked over her shoulder through the window and saw the couple on the couch. The moment came to bear upon her exactly like that, with that great hush, with a surprising, silent force.

In that same instant, Johannes Meyer looked up from the couch and their eyes met, and it was as though she could see everything that was inside the boy. And he saw her too (she knew it!) and together they confirmed something they'd always known but only now remembered.

AT OTTO KESSLER'S COFFEE HOUSE IN TAUBENSTRAßE

A portly young man came one evening and proposed that each one of us was a living premonition and proof (in the ever-present) of the past and the future fused together.

'We are a weld,' this man named Krüger said, 'of every event and eventuality.'

Nobody listening responded, or seemed to understand (Krüger could tell by their eyes; he'd had this before and in other places). Disappointed, he cleared his throat and again willed brightness into his voice. It was particularly noisy at Otto's on Taubenstraße that Wednesday night.

'Déjà vu,' Krüger said. '*Déjà*, it means *already*: the sense that something has already happened before, though it's also happening *now*. Who hasn't felt it?'

Again, nothing.

His brightness dimmed. Krüger preferred to bounce off people when he spoke, draw up quickly against their arguments, derive an intuitive direction and logic from the to-and-fro. Otherwise, in the lagging silence, he had a tendency to grow flustered and confuse himself, lose confidence, his arguments then clattering around in his mind like a shod horse spooked on cobblestones. Which was exactly what had happened to him the previous year, during his disastrous oral presentation at the University of Jena, when he'd been denied a degree.

He took a deep breath, composed himself.

'Time isn't a straight line and it doesn't travel a distance,' Krüger said. 'Our lives are merely remaindered embodiments of this false notion, anxious and afflicted because time is *imposed*. For truly, and we all know it, there is no time*line*. Our lives don't actually *go* anywhere. We are always *here*, wherever we are.' He held out his arms. 'Where is there to go?'

Somebody called out, 'Home!'

Laughter.

Another voice: 'But haven't I been there before?'

They were gathered around a couple of tables in a corner of the coffee house. Otto's on Taubenstraße was full of students, young men, older men, lonely men, wounded soldiers, philosophers without formal qualification, cold street dwellers clutching a few begged pfennigs, poets. They smiled. They were enjoying this fellow.

'The truth is that we churn in a state of circular intertwining,' Krüger said, persisting, nothing to lose now, 'caught in a ceaseless and immutable folding, like . . . like cards shuffled by the gods. There are only so many combinations.'

Johannes Meyer leaned forward on his elbows, tried to listen, but the man's arguments were difficult to follow with the growing chatter. Still, something had caught like a hook into his feelings. This man called Krüger was awkward and Johannes could sense how he'd alienated himself from the crowd there at Otto's, and maybe that was all it was, the hook: that Johannes knew how the man felt and could hear the truth in his voice. He believed him.

'The rigid retrospectives of age,' Krüger said, 'the prison of numbered years, those most tenacious and insinuating agents of measurement, are an illusion. They draw a single straight line through life, but cannot by nature contain the whole of the movement encompassed. Life is not unfurling in a line, but rather being spun, constantly, around and around our voluptuous Mother Earth, who is herself simultaneously turning, turning!'

Krüger was twenty-four, pear-shaped like his mother, with narrow sloping shoulders adding emphasis to the thighs and buttocks. His blue eyes had often earned him a second look, but so far he'd been in love only once. He claimed to be from a small town in Westphalia, but nobody had ever heard of it, and later, when he left, the regulars at Otto Kessler's on Taubenstraße agreed that his accent wasn't even close to Westphalian.

'And so,' Krüger said, 'thereby, our conclusion: the inevitability of passing through where all and one have already been before and, in fact, must and will be, forever.'

LOVE IS RECOGNITION

Johannes Meyer couldn't recall everything Krüger said that night, nor did he understand much of what he remembered; but now, as he looked up from the couch and saw Elisabeth von Hoffmann's face in the window, framed in warm light, pale gold, beautiful, eternal, some impression of the man's words made him suddenly think: Yes!

Their youthful eyes met and exchanged the moment, unrestrained, fluid, full. Their youthful eyes held and locked together. Johannes Meyer had been here before, that was the feeling, and he knew the girl, or must have known her once, or would do so, or . . . or, otherwise, why this overwhelming sense of her?

'Listen,' Krüger had said finally at Otto's that night, though by now only Johannes and two or three others were listening to him. 'The heart, not the mind, sets all criteria for truth, and love is its ingenium. And love is recognition: *recognoscere, cognoscere*, to know. Yes? All that is behind us, and all that is before us, is here, always, already, to know. You know it. You already know what's true. You already know.'

Johannes Meyer looked up and he *knew*. And the girl in the window, she knew it too. And though they neither had any idea what it was that should be known, the revelation that something was known and could be known seemed more than enough.

LOVE IS LOSS

Beatrice pulled the boy down and held him tightly in her arms. She closed her eyes, so the world was as small as it could be.

She'd noticed, seen it straight off, Johannes looking away from her then; she knew, she'd seen what had come into his eyes and felt his departure keenly, his heart, his presence, everything dissolving. And never mind the cruel moment, that it was exactly a betrayal, unkind and unforgivable. This wasn't the injury complete. It was her failure too, her self-loathing, that she couldn't contain the boy, even after lifting her skirts. It wasn't enough, was never enough, no matter how much she hoped it would be.

Her father had said to her once: 'It's what you bring upon yourself.'

Johannes had also felt the moment between them as it died, but the face of the girl in the window had refused to fade from his eyes and now it was impossible to recover what had been with Beatrice in the moments before.

She stood up from the couch and smoothed her skirts. She tucked loose strands of hair behind her ears, pulled at her sleeves, fussed at her clothes. She looked everywhere except directly at Johannes.

'Beatrice,' he said.

'You have to go now,' she said firmly. 'You can't be here.'

They were in the home of Claus von Rolt, whom Beatrice worked for when she wasn't at Otto's coffee house. Here she cleaned and mopped and dusted, sometimes kept his bed warm, too. She'd known Rolt was going to be away for the afternoon.

'See you, Johannes.'

'Wait . . .'

But Beatrice turned away, went to the front door and stepped outside. Then the door closed and she was gone.

And that's all we'll ever know about her. She has slipped off our map.

EELS

On the other side of Berlin, in an empty storehouse in Königstadt that smelled strongly of manure, straw and damp flagstones, Claus von Rolt was with the American, Wesley Lewis Jr, and his Surinamese Negro companion, introduced simply as Mr Hendrik.

Claus von Rolt stood with his arms crossed, staring at a briny oak barrel of dark sludge. He was disappointed with everything today: with the American, with the barrel, with Bonaparte at the gate. He reminded himself of his personal dictum—that expectations in life should always be cold, contained and disposable—but it didn't help.

'Genuine New World electrificated eels,' Wesley Lewis Jr had said, levering off the barrel lid with a small iron bar. 'You can look, but just don't dare touch 'em.'

Rolt was still staring at the barrel. He watched an oily bubble slowly dome on the surface and expand for a moment, then pop, exhausted. Of the six eels slopping around in there, one was dead and floated belly up. The others slid their slimy bodies over it every now and then, but appeared so sluggish that death was surely imminent for them also. The American's asking price was offensive for so damaged a cargo.

Still, Rolt wanted them. There were collectors willing to pay exorbitantly, and there were people to gift and impress, as always, in the effort to slip open sluice gates and direct the flows of profit. Rarity and exotica was his game, and even bruised in careless handling (even dead) it would always attract good money.

The Negro, Mr Hendrik, watched silently, leaning off his lame leg.

'Mr von Rolt?' Wesley Lewis Jr said. He could never remember if you were meant to say the *von*.

'I'll pay half,' Claus von Rolt said.

The American grinned, but not because anything was funny. Three months to get here and now this pompous

Prussian wanted to haggle. Jesus, but what a prick. He felt the twitch he'd recently acquired return to the corner of his left eye. In that deranged little spasm, all he'd endured: the steaming, insect-plagued forests of Surinam, the crossing of roiling, pirate-infested seas on that bloated slug the *Alfons*, then the volatile borders all through Europe, harassed by murderous highwaymen and fleeced by counts and princes to pass their roads, and now, the sudden walking blind into a war and Bonaparte's two-hundred-thousand-strong stinking, looting, cutthroat Grande goddamn Armée on the march in the same direction. And everybody wanting to know, everywhere they went: What's in the barrel, son?

And his companion, the Negro, speaking barely a word the whole time, except to say 'water' now and then, as though Wesley Lewis Jr needed reminding to replenish the barrel in order to keep the eel sons-of-bitches alive and kicking.

'How about you stand there and watch,' he'd say, inserting the tap at the bottom of the barrel to drain it, after some hours trying to find fresh water in a dead village somewhere, skinny dogs barking at him, cannon thunder and smoke on the horizon. 'Make sure I do it properly.' But the Negro never bit.

Wesley Lewis Jr walked slowly over to the barrel and picked up the lid that was leaning against it. He turned the greasy wheel in his hands, looking it over, then placed the lid carefully on top of the barrel, crouching a little to check the alignment. He gave it some attention, took his time, made sure it was straight. Then he stood back, put his hands on his hips.

'The day we set off into the forests of Surinam,' he said, 'the barge nearly sank after hitting a reef of sunken trees at the river edge. The port bow plunged down and we took a big slurp of water and all the slave paddlers panicked, stood up and rushed around the deck like a bunch of chickens, sent the barge tilting even more. The Negroes can't swim, of course, and naturally one of them fell in. While he thrashed about drowning, a giant, fifteen-foot caiman woke up from lying in the sun and slipped off the bank into the river. For a few seconds you could see the crust of black mud on his back melt and billow out into the water like smoke, but then he disappeared deeper and it was just the sunlight tinkling on the ripples he'd made. The boy was still drowning and a couple of Negroes were trying to reach out to him with their paddles, all the rest of them were yelling, gibbering and gesticulating—it was enough to wish 'em all drowned. And then, just like that, the boy went under, gone. Everything quiet.' Wesley Lewis Jr wiped his hands down his pants. 'We kept watching the spot where he'd been, waiting, waiting, but nothing happened, it was like the whole thing was a dream. And then there was this great almighty splash and the surface broke and we saw the boy again. Only now the caiman had clamped his enormous jaws down on his shoulder, and was trying to wrap himself around the boy, and began rolling him, both of them spinning like logs. The boy's face, Jesus—screaming terror! I'll tell you, Mr *von* Rolt, there isn't anything more obscene or sickening than the sight of that beast's buttery, slimy-scaled belly. There's a reason why God put him so close to the ground.'

'Herr Lewis,' Claus von Rolt said. 'I think we should—'

'We clear the snag, we go on, fifty miles of river,' Wesley Lewis Jr said, cutting the Prussian off, 'then a four-day trek to get to where the eels are, one man short. You ever experience the wild forests of the New World, Mr von Rolt? Swarms of mosquitoes, the even bigger *zancudos*, and these little bastards the French call *bête-rouge*, make you itch to kingdom come. And then there's the *chegoes*, which love to crawl into your boots and burrow into the skin between your toes and lay their eggs. Of course, the snakes, caimans, jaguars, all that. I could go on, but I understand you're a busy man. When we finally got back to my employer's sugar plantation—that's Captain van der Velde, whom I believe you've had correspond-ences with—well, he wants to test something out. Before we barrel up the eels, he wants to see what happens if you touch one. So he orders one of his slaves—an older man, scarred all over from the whip—Captain van der Velde orders him to pick one up out of the barrel.'

Wesley Lewis Jr slapped the barrel wood.

'Of course, the Negro's *reluctant*, but he's got no choice. Trembling, he slowly reaches in and then, before he can even get a decent grip on the slimy bastard, receives such a jolt that he falls back onto the ground as though he's been shot. Then the captain orders another slave to push the eel onto the man's body, which he does, terrified, with a stick, and then we all watch it stretch along the Negro's body and begin to pulse and change colour, and the Negro sets to twitching and shaking. His black heart's already stopped, but he keeps twitching and shaking until the eel is spent. Then the creature rested a moment before slithering away.'

Wesley Lewis Jr paused. 'One of these eels, sir, right here in this barrel. A man killer.'

'Half,' Claus von Rolt said again.

Wesley Lewis Jr frowned and was about to reply when Mr Hendrik took him by the arm. Turning to the Prussian, the Negro bowed his head a little, blinked his eyes in the slow, sleepy way that Wesley Lewis Jr couldn't stand, and said, 'We accept your offer.'

GUESTS

The family lawyer Seidlitz was there when Elisabeth von Hoffmann returned home with Günther Jagelman. She couldn't stand Seidlitz and mostly wished he'd fall under a horse. Hearing the man's voice as they entered the house, she turned into the sitting room and walked to the large window that looked out over the street. The house wasn't far from Unter den Linden and people were everywhere still, passing by below the window, heading towards Napoleon. She watched them, indifferent, could only think of the boy she'd seen.

From down the hall, her aunt's voice. 'Elisabeth!'

She rolled her eyes, whispered, *God*, and then composed herself. She went to see what Aunt Margaretha wanted now.

'Must I call you twice?'

'I'm sorry, Aunt, I didn't hear you.'

Aunt Margaretha shook her head, a quick, irritated movement that wobbled her old jowls and jangled her long silver earrings, hanging low on doughy lobes. She was on the settee, heavy and spread out, the lawyer Seidlitz beside her on a chair, and Günther standing nearby, silent as always.

'And how was Napoleon?' Margaretha said. 'Did you give him my regards?'

'Of course, Aunt, just as you wished. We had schnapps together.'

Margaretha scoffed. The lawyer proceeded to unbuckle two thin straps on a satchel in his lap. He removed a document scroll and laid it on the satchel. Seidlitz was short, fat and tightly bound in unfashionable clothes, still preferring to display his plump calves by wearing trousers with leggings and high-heeled shoes. He crossed his legs and bounced his foot lightly up and down, pointing the toes.

'We are to have a guest,' Margaretha said. 'A Frenchman.'

'Who?'

'Général Michel François Fourés,' the lawyer Seidlitz said, unfurling and holding up the document that had arrived earlier from the French military administration.

'Dear God!' Margaretha said. 'What will people say? Serving the enemy!'

'We are not the only ones, Frau von Hoffmann,' the lawyer said. 'Most of the French officers are being billeted with the finest families across the city.'

'My life has been cruel and unrelenting!' Margaretha said. 'And persists!'

Elisabeth's aunt longed only to return to her bed, where she spent most of her time these days. For this sentence of loneliness, and for her ageing spinsterhood, she explicitly blamed her family, and most particularly Elisabeth's father, her brother, whose face she saw each time she looked upon the rosy bloom of her young niece. She blamed Elisabeth's mother, too. They'd both died young so inconsiderately and burdened her with their loathsome child.

'It will not be forever, Frau von Hoffmann,' the lawyer Seidlitz said. 'We will endure and soon prosper once again.'

Aunt Margaretha began to weep. Günther reached across and patted her shoulder. The lawyer joined in on the other side.

Elisabeth said, 'Can I go now?'

THE VULTURE, OTHER SPECIMENS, AND THE SEASHELL

Sarcoramphus papa, on a heavy wooden plinth; scaly bald head of red, black and mandarin yellow, hooked red-orange beak beneath its grisly caruncle, enormous black-and-white wings, kinked like giant arrowheads and held aloft, as though the bird were about to hop over the furniture on its huge, blunt talons. Its eye followed Johannes Meyer, the eye disconcertingly alive. He moved past it, at a distance.

The room was spacious, opulently furnished, painted vases and cut-glass bowls and silver trinkets everywhere. A clock ticked and eased the silence.

Johannes walked through a doorway. The adjoining room was darker, cooler. Cabinet cases, apothecary shelves, books to the ceiling. The smell of leather, tobacco, dust, something acidic.

In pale honey-coloured box frames on the walls, leaves, pressed flowers, butterflies and beetles, and gruesome fine-haired spiders with black marble eyes, all set in scrupulous rows, pinned and named. In specimen drawers with thin brass handles and Latin designations on yellow card, fossils and rocks and molten drops of amber, perfect mosquitoes and muscle-legged grasshoppers entombed inside, waiting. In glass cabinet displays, gleaming river stones and shards of crystal, everything arranged in perfect themes of shading, lightest to darkest, pastel pinks and watery blues, dusty reds and creamy greens; and birds' eggs too, smallest to largest, grey and black-speckled, blue, pink and white.

Johannes Meyer went from one display to the other. Opened drawers and closed them. With his fingertips traced the corrugated coils of baby snakes in jars of yellow liquid. For the second time today, he experienced the feeling of having been somewhere before.

On a mahogany side table he found a large seashell. It was smooth and polished, white orange and bright, even there in the dimness of the room, as though sunlight and the shimmering of tropical waters were stored in its curled, half-closed porcelain flower. He picked it up, and just as he pressed the rounded lips of the shell to his ear, exactly then, he heard the front door snap its latch and creak open.

Beatrice coming back? He listened.

On Unter den Linden, the Emperor waved to the crowd and there was a cheer that spread out into the surrounding streets and entered the front door of Claus von Rolt's house, even reached into the room where Johannes Meyer stood. He held his breath while his old life overlapped with the new, the seams stitched by the hoof-taps of Bonaparte's horse.

'Life is an uncertain navigation of transcendent uncertainty,' Krüger had said. 'It begs only a scrutiny of the heart.'

Not Beatrice, but three men walked into Claus von Rolt's house.

YOUR MONEY OR YOUR LIFE

Wesley Lewis Jr was small and slightly built, as though the designation at the end of his name had manifested itself physically.

His father was taller and broader and closer to God, too, a preacher in South Carolina with flagellatory tendencies towards his son (switches, belts, whips, riding crops). He daily cleansed the boy of sin on behalf of the mother, who'd long abandoned them to whore out her comforts for corn liquor in Georgia, in Alabama, in Louisiana last they heard. Still,

Wesley Lewis Jr hated neither mother nor father as much as he hated the Surinamese Negro, his companion, Mr Hendrik.

There in the storehouse with the cocky Prussian waiting, and the electrical eels half dead in the barrel and Mr Hendrik's hand still on his arm, Wesley Lewis Jr looked into the Negro's burnt molasses eyes, those huge, round, voodoo eyes, animal and cannibal. The crippled slave so much older than his years, in frockcoat and buckled shoes, for Christ's sake.

'And what would your master say to such a price?' Wesley Lewis Jr said from between his clenched teeth.

'Leave it done,' Mr Hendrik said.

Wesley Lewis Jr pulled his arm free. Since they'd left Paramaribo together with their rare merchandise, he'd been thinking of it, how he might murder the Negro, be done with him and pocket the purse, make his way back to America. But he'd become fearful, at times even believed that Mr Hendrik knew exactly the thoughts percolating in his mind. Black magic, the *obia*, oh yes, he knew the sly, shifty Negro was versed in such things. He'd seen it. Like the night in Havana on the way, in one of the stinking lanes leading from the docks to the taverns, Mr Hendrik and himself suddenly surrounded by three men, one armed with a pistol.

'*Entregar o morir!*'

Even with the limp, a broken body, in a flash the Negro had slipped a knife and slashed the wrist of the gunman. Before the pistol had clattered on the ground, the second man clutched at his throat and collapsed. The third ran, desperate for his life, followed by the bleeding gunman, crying out, *'El diablo! El diablo!'*

And that later midnight, docked in Rotterdam, Wesley Lewis Jr asleep in his hammock, then waking with a jolt and Mr Hendrik there above him, staring down, his bloodshot eyes glowing moon-yellow in the dark; and then, in a blink, gone! Only the creaking of briny timbers, the hull groaning, burdened, the dark ghouled. He was shaken for days. How often had the Negro watched him sleeping? What had he read in Wesley Lewis Jr's dreams?

Josephine. He must surely have seen Josephine.

A most deceitful and murderous Negro!

Claus von Rolt said, 'Then we are in accord?'

Mr Hendrik nodded.

'Good,' Rolt said and indicated for his assistant to take care of the barrel of eels. 'We can take my carriage and complete our transactions over brandy in my home.'

LIQUORICE

A native woman called Susanna had retrieved the shell for her husband, Georg Eberhard Rumpf, who collected plants and seashells and worked for the Dutch East India Company. This was in Ambon, in the Moluccan Archipelago, about a century ago. She'd dived expertly through twenty feet of water as clear as sky to pluck it from the sea-floor. Maybe it was already a thousand years old, maybe more. However old it was, hers were the first human hands ever to touch it. And Johannes Meyer's the last! In between, it had traced an invisible route to Rolt's mahogany side table (as had the mahogany).

On Unter den Linden, Bonaparte casually slipped a piece of liquorice into his mouth; and here, three men walked in to surprise Johannes, holding Susanna's rare shell in his hands. Shocked, frightened, he dropped it and watched open-mouthed as it shattered into pieces across the floor.

HOW GREAT IT IS TO RUN

Mr Hendrik didn't try to stop the boy. In fact, he moved a little to the left, out of the way of the door, and let the boy run past.

Claus von Rolt lunged, cried, 'Stop!' but couldn't get hold of him. The boy burst outside and into the street.

'Why didn't you grab him?' Wesley Lewis Jr said with disgust. He quickly ran off after the boy and Rolt followed.

Mr Hendrik stood in the doorway and watched. His face was inscrutable, but inside he urged the boy on.

Run.

He felt the flutter of nerves in his own legs, even the useless one. The dull ache there sharpened, a memory triggered, a twitch from the past.

Run, boy.

A CHILDHOOD

Mr Hendrik was twelve years old, thin and long-legged.

His own uncle wielded the knife and four slaves held his limbs, splayed out over the ground, and there was another hand that pushed his face down, so that he thought they meant to drown him in the mud. His miserable uncle with the blade, given the task and no choice about it, the blade blunt and crude and purposely so, sawing the boy's leg with gruesome imprecision, through skin and flesh and then at last the tendon above and at the back of the ankle, hacked and severed with a whip snap. The boy howled and thought he was going to die.

When he finished, the uncle wiped the blade on the grass. This wasn't the first or last hamstrung Negro he'd midwife. And he'd told the boy too, warned him before and shaken him as he did so: *Don't run, you fool. There's nowhere to run.*

But Mr Hendrik hadn't planned on a destination. It was enough just to run, in any direction. It was at the core of him and thoughtless, like life.

POET

The crowds were packed into every street, every lane. Johannes crashed into them and tried to push through, but not even a crack opened to him. As he struggled, a hand grabbed his shoulder and pulled him back, threw him roughly to the ground. A French soldier.

Claus von Rolt's voice: 'He's the one!'

Wesley Lewis Jr stood beside him, hands on his knees, looking up but breathing hard from the pursuit.

All Johannes could see were legs and boots. He tried to get to his feet but was kicked in the stomach, hard enough that all the air was punched out of his lungs. Then he was slapped across the head and dragged along the cobblestones by his coat collar. The coat ripped at the shoulder stitching and one of his shoes came off.

Somebody said, 'What'd he do?'

'A rioter!'

'No!' Johannes said. He couldn't believe what was happening to him. He wasn't thinking of the seashell, of being caught in the house; it was that they'd already tried to sweep him up before, the authorities, gather him in their net, his friends too, for war, for death, for the Fatherland. He was a poet, not a soldier, never!

Johannes was pulled up onto his feet. Two French soldiers had him by the arms and more of them stood around. Some of the crowd had heard the commotion and they turned now to see Johannes in the hands of the French. Their compatriot and the enemy. A whisper began, more heads turned, and then a few people approached the soldiers.

The French, battle-worn but sharp to the changing atmosphere, closed ranks. Muskets were unslung and bayonets pointed. More of the crowd turned, more faces frowned, the whispers grew louder. A young man jumped out and waved his fist.

'Verdammte Französische fotzen!'

The blow from the stock of a soldier's musket knocked him to the ground.

Now the crowd hesitated, shocked. The moment shaped itself to each individual fear. The French soldiers, who'd marched hundreds of miles and knew every kind of fear there was, waited, firm, resolute. Johannes raised his head, grimacing in pain, saw his countrymen step back and dissolve into the larger crowd behind them, still waving and cheering for Napoleon Bonaparte.

AGITATOR

Twelve days later, Sous-lieutenant Hubert Pessac, the new prison commandant in Berlin, ran his finger down a list of names written in the ledger open before him on the desk. The list recorded everyone arrested in the city on 27 October 1806. There were twenty-two names in total, written in a slanting script. He dragged his finger down and found the next entry.

Meyer, Johannes, eighteen, Hirtengaße.

Pessac called for the man, and his sergeant went out to bring the prisoner up from the cells.

'Make sure you tell them you're a deserter,' a man called Wolfie said. He was the only man in the cells who'd bothered to speak to Johannes. He didn't have many teeth left but liked to smile. The boy reminded him of a brother, long gone now and buried in the mud of some forgotten battlefield.

'But they'll know,' Johannes said.

'Just tell them. They'll put you in the army if they think you can hold a musket. Then at least there's a chance to run. Otherwise it's the galleys and an oar at your guts until your beard reaches your balls. That's if you don't die first and they throw you overboard. Right?'

'But I didn't do anything!'

'That doesn't matter anymore, my friend. Best forget it.'

The day everybody went out to see Napoleon Bonaparte enter the city, Wolfie had been caught breaking into houses. His wife had sewed long pockets inside his coat and Wolfie had filled them with bread, brandy, sausage, silk handker-chiefs, jewellery, silver cutlery. He told Johannes it had been a grand day, the best day ever, until they caught him. 'I was greedy,' he said. 'I should've gone home after the first few houses. But what a day! I couldn't resist. It felt so good to be rich.'

He slapped Johannes on the back. 'Trust me, boy.'

'But what will I say? I don't know anything about the army.'

'Tell them you deserted from the Puttkammer Infantry Regiment. Number forty. Auerstedt. Got it?'

'They might check.'

'Be confident! What's there to check? They always need soldiers.'

When the sergeant came and took Johannes away, Wolfie called after him, 'Look ahead, son. Dead straight ahead. The past is over.'

In Pessac's office, the sergeant pushed Johannes towards the desk. His wrists were shackled and so were his ankles.

'Stand there.'

Pessac sniffed a lavender-scented handkerchief at his wrist, tucked inside the cuff of his jacket.

'Proceed,' he said.

The sergeant began to narrate the circumstances of the boy's arrest. Johannes quickly interrupted.

'Sir, I did nothing wrong!' he said. 'I'm innocent of all charges!'

'Silence!'

'It's a misunderstanding!'

The sergeant punched Johannes in the kidneys.

Pessac held up his hand and nodded. The details really had no bearing on things. While Johannes Meyer groaned and kneeled into the pain ripping through him, Pessac dipped his quill into the inkpot. He wrote *agitator* into the last blank column.

Johannes managed to look up. He knew for certain now that everything was over. He wasn't going home. The realisation came coldly and, to his surprise, with strange relief.

'Sir, I'm sorry,' he said. There was nothing to lose now. 'Sir . . . I'm a deserter.'

The prison commandant frowned. 'From where?'

'Puttkammer Infantry Regiment, sir. Number forty. Auerstedt.'

Pessac cleared his throat, took a deep breath. Really, they wasted so much of his time. He'd have to blot out what he'd already written. Fine. He did so, and changed *agitator* to *deserter.* Then in another column he wrote *4e Régiment Étrangers.* Then he waved the boy and the sergeant away.

GODS

They'd also watched Bonaparte's victory parade, as they watched many things in the world and would always watch them, and (among others) they'd picked Johannes Meyer out. It mostly always happened like that, for no reason and at random. Probably they were bored with Bonaparte; he'd had such a good run since being plucked out of Corsica, and here was just more of the same pomp. Everyone knows the gods love a good joke, and look ... They grinned and nodded between themselves and then pointed down at the crowd, made more random selections: him, her, her, him et cetera. Choices made, they whipped up the sticky tendrils of fate and loosed the surging winds of change (those puff-cheeked cherubs) and young Johannes Meyer felt a shiver down his back.

And then the gods took a well-deserved afternoon nap.

All that's left for us are the incomplete maps, to conjecture and argue their scale.

BOOK II

THE PEAKS OF SUCCESS

Général de Brigade Michel François Fourés had given up on being received by the Emperor.

At the Battle of Jena, and then leading his cuirassiers against Prussian forces along the Isserstadt–Vierzehnheiligen line, he'd forced General Hohenlohe's troops into a wild retreat, all the way beyond Gross Romstadt and into the dewy Capellendorf Valley, the Prussians abandoning artillery, arms and supplies as they ran, surrendering by the hundreds. No matter, it seemed, this success. Instead of an audience with the Emperor, instead of orders to pursue the fleeing Prussians and their king (instead of *honours*), he'd been assigned administrative duties in Berlin.

The général was aware they all disliked him—Berthier, Soult, Lanne, Ney and Davout, the marvellous maréchals of this Prussian campaign (and before that the Italian, and before that the Austrian, and before that all the other campaigns). They had the Emperor's ear. A ring of whisperers. The further up the ranks of the Grande Armée Fourés had risen, the more he'd had to contend with their politics and manoeuvring.

Finally, it seemed, he'd reached his summit. There was no place else for him to go.

Administrative duties.

Of course, it didn't help that his younger brother was a royalist who'd fled to England after the Revolution. For years now Étienne had published scurrilous pieces against Bonaparte in the *Courier de Londres*. It was said the Emperor hated Étienne Fourés *the most* of all the exiled royalist writers. Maybe, Général Fourés thought, maybe it's true that I've done better than could be expected. If only Letizia hadn't gone and left him, also.

Beautiful, young, cushioned Letizia.

'I'm a lady,' she'd said. 'And I refuse to make love under grey canvas any longer. Surrounded by indecent soldiery!'

She'd often accompanied Fourés on campaign and it had never bothered her before. Then again, Captain Philippe Ducasse had never been around before either, handsome and dashing and just returned from distinguished service in the West Indies. A young man on the rise. Letizia knew a good bachelor when she saw one, especially in the wild like this, so to speak, away from tenacious Parisian competition. She also knew that Fourés's wife refused him a divorce. And no doubt the young captain's tent was bright and warm, anything but grey.

The général's carriage pulled up in the street. His aide-de-camp leaned across and looked out of the window.

'The von Hoffmann house, Général,' he said.

SUFFERING IS ONLY A SMALL PART OF THE TRUTH

Krüger sat in a corner at Otto Kessler's coffee house on Taubenstraße. His notebook was open on the table in front of him. On a fresh page, he'd written:

All that can be known is there to know and is already known.

Only courage remains for us to author.

Courage the deed to this knowing.

But that was yesterday. All last night and this morning, too, he'd been unable to continue. Every word he wrote embarrassed him. It was all nonsense. And now he'd drunk too much coffee and his stomach burned. Berlin was a disappointment. Maybe the carriage out in the morning would jolt his thinking, break in some new ideas. For now, it was like being curled up and nailed into a box.

In Magdeburg, before she died, Hilde had said to him, 'You think too hard, Heinrich.' With her illness, her criticisms were sharper, without prologue, and they stung him. 'But it's not in there, my love,' she said. 'Everything is outside, all around you.'

Krüger frowned. There was that tone again, loving, sincere, calmly intelligent. Unimpeachable. He said, 'What is?'

'Everything you could wish to know.'

He rubbed his face with both hands; held them there, pressed and traced the ridges of bone over his eyes.

'It doesn't have to be so painful,' she said. 'Suffering is only a small part of the truth.'

'Thank you, Fräulein Philosophia,' Krüger said through his fingers. (How he regretted that childish tone now!)

Heinrich and Hilde. Hilde and Heinrich. Like the title of a play: a romance or tragedy, or a comedy perhaps.

She was a thousand times more gifted, more brilliant, more deserving of life's riches, even now when she was gone.

BLOODLINES

The Tricolore flapped brightly over Charlottenburg Palace.

Inside, the Prussians were grim and lost. Their good King Frederick was gone, fled to Osterode with Queen Louisa and a thin cabinet of ministers. Their hearts ached for their king and they moved dejectedly among the striding French. Up and down the magnificent hallways of the palace and inside the magisterial rooms and chambers, the French! Enemy messengers, aides-de-camp, adjutants, soldiers and officers, instantly familiar, right at home, moved about with purpose, ignored them. Salt in the wounds. And yet, even in their whispering, defeated huddles, each man desired to see their conqueror in the flesh. To be tied to history, to have a story to tell their grandchildren. They looked up at every sound of footsteps and click of door latches, hopeful for a glimpse. He's here, somewhere! Right now! they all thought. Napoleon!

The loyal, the shamed but not defeated (the truly loyal), were of course appalled by their fickle compatriots. They held the fight to the French. They'd hidden the wine and the brandy. They'd taken the firewood away in carts (as much as they could shift in the short time they had) and they'd stolen the candles and chamber-pots and the sugar, and they'd opened all the windows to let the cold evening air into the vast palace hallways and rooms. They'd be damned if Bonaparte would pass any comfortable days here.

Their heroism, inevitably, amounted to not much. They were only a small group. Most of their fickle compatriots thought them absurd and idiotic. The French paid no attention to their childish sabotage. They had plenty of brandy and pissed out the windows.

At the palace now, it was gossip and rumours at their zenith, every subject imaginable. The future of Prussia, the fate of Europe, the Emperor's luncheon menu, his favourite cologne. A chambermaid had seen his penis.

'Small,' she'd said. 'Like a little snail lost its shell.'

Every keyhole an eye.

Bonaparte had instructed the fires be lit in his chambers (the palace was like a tomb, he said). He was still waiting for someone to come. His fearful staff eventually broke the furniture and piled the mahogany splinters high. In the early morning he would depart for Poland.

The Empress Josephine had written that she was pleased for him, his great triumph. She'd sent him more liquorice from the *confiseur* on rue du Faubourg Saint-Honoré. Paris was grey without him, she wrote. And, no, she wasn't pregnant.

INTRODUCTIONS

Günther Jagelman and the von Hoffmann family lawyer Seidlitz greeted Général Fourés and his aide-de-camp, Christophe Bergerard. Aunt Margaretha refused to come out of her bedroom (she would spend the next few weeks there). As they stood awkwardly in the entrance hall, soldiers brought the général's things inside from the carriage and piled them on the parquet floor.

'Welcome, Général,' Seidlitz said.

'Thank you, Monsieur.'

'I must apologise, Général, for Frau von Hoffmann's absence. She is suffering from the *grippe* and has taken to her bed.'

'I trust our presence will not make her suffer for too long.'

Seidlitz smiled. 'Yes . . . or rather, no, not at all, Général!'

Fourés looked around, impressed by the wealth and obvious standing of his hosts. Among the portraits and landscapes on the walls, he noticed a Van Dyck and, nearby, a Terborch as well. He walked over to take a closer look (it was *The Paternal Admonition*, magnificent). He admired the painting and wondered how long it would take the Emperor's plunderer, Vivant Denon, to come help himself and add the treasure to his Musée Napoléon. The man could smell a Vermeer at two hundred yards. (He'd already begun the removal of the quadriga over the Brandenburg Gate, as per Bonaparte's wishes.) Fourés contemplated whether he shouldn't tell these von Hoffmanns to hide their rare paintings, quickly now, but then decided to mind his own business.

'Our chambers?' his aide-de-camp Bergerard said.

Old Günther extended his arm. 'This way, please.'

Elisabeth von Hoffmann met them in the hallway, where the lawyer Seidlitz introduced her.

'Mademoiselle,' the général said. He took her hand, bowed his head and kissed it. 'I hope we will not intrude upon your lives too much.'

'How can you not?' Elisabeth said.

'Then we must compensate you, Mademoiselle.'

Elisabeth said nothing, gave Fourés a shallow, mocking curtsey and continued down the hall.

By God, the général thought. A beauty!

As Elisabeth walked off, she was thinking that Général Fourés had paid much attention to the styling of his thinning chestnut hair. It was combed upwards and swept into soft curling waves, all of it together swirled to an impressive height, ensuring he was marginally taller than her. Licked points fringed his forehead and delicate wisps hooked his ears, just like on a Roman bust.

So he was vain (it's not a sin, she thought). But she'd liked the sound of his voice, she supposed (did she really?). His teeth were clean and the shape of his mouth wasn't cruel. She thought his brown eyes softened the otherwise haughty arch of his brows. He was older, that was true, and when he kissed her hand she'd caught a glimpse of the pink shininess of his scalp—but, then, nobody was perfect.

BERLIN'S A DOG!

What he wanted was a black woman.

No. He wanted Josephine.

Wesley Lewis Jr's first sight of her: it was just after luncheon, his head pounding, soused and heavy in the gut, swaying beneath the hot, searing sky. Numb inside the cushioning sweet wet green of the surrounding sugarcane.

He saw her disembark from a barge on the river, a stunningly beautiful dark mulatto, barefoot in a pale blue European dress, a frilled rose-red umbrella in her hand, her arm hooked in Mr Hendrik's. As they walked, Wesley Lewis Jr watched the Negro pack, damp down, light and then hand her a long wooden pipe, which she began to smoke, smiling, giggling, pressing her head to his shoulder, affectionate and loving. They'd been in town, a rare privilege, and she was his half-sister, barely fourteen years, and Captain van der Velde's mistress. Wesley Lewis Jr had heard of her, and now understood the talk. Every desire he'd ever felt in his life that moment poured into the image of her. The beautiful slave Josephine.

Josephine of Surinam.

He'd bedded an abundance of black flesh in his time, from South Carolina to Cuba, from the Caribbean islands to the plateaus of Brazil, and in every shade of light and every shade of night, but none were like this vision here before him. The sun!

But she was half the world away. So, right now, Wesley Lewis Jr, no question, would pay double (triple!) for a black woman. And he'd pay for heat and sweat and sugarcane liquor, too.

Not a chance.

Christ Almighty, but Berlin was a dog!

Only one more night, he told himself. We're leaving in the morning.

He poured more schnapps into his coffee cup, splashing some onto the table. Through narrowed, drunken eyes he watched the girls serving.

Nothing like the girls he knew. Those Surinam girls, van der Velde's girls, deep into the night, deep into the dark, the table heaving, the candlelight, a ship's hold of gorging and laughing and shouting and singing and fucking. Those girls.

Van der Velde's girls. Beautiful Negresses, brown angel mulattoes, feasts, dark nipples and gleaming dark flesh, gleaming, molasses under the moon.

Kill-devil liquor, and heat, blue, green: impenetrable green. Remember the slave hanging from the tree?

Wesley Lewis Jr had just arrived at the plantation, first day, off the barge from Paramaribo and still wobbly after the

45

sea voyage from South Carolina and there he was, the Negro, swinging gently in the breeze, an iron hook pushed into his ribs, hands tied behind his back, his face anguish carved out of stone.

'Still not dead,' somebody said. Still not dead, two days later. 'Maybe tomorrow,' they said. 'You never can guess it.'

The serving girl at Otto's came by. 'More coffee?'

'*Nein!*' Wesley Lewis Jr's bladder was tight as a drum, but he wouldn't get up yet. He had capacity, by God he did, but enough damn coffee.

At Captain van der Velde's the world stopped spinning. He had capacity! He held on. You couldn't fall off if you held on. He'd *never* fallen off.

Everything floated: the food on the plates, the chairs in the room and the candlelight like illuminated smoke. The black beauties in embroidered Indian skirts, wrists tinkling with bracelets of polished stone and shell, blue and red, chains of gold and silver looped over their breasts and honey-yellow flowers in their hair, pollen-dusted. Wesley Lewis Jr would think of his preacher father and laugh. Preaching for pennies in Charleston.

'Berlin's a dog!' he cried out.

A cockroach scampered across the table: gone by the time he smacked his hand down. Wasn't that his first deal? That Catalan banker, the closet coleopterist, and the fat wife who'd wasted no time cashing in when he died. A priceless collection of six thousand beetles, painstakingly acquired over a lifetime, collected and meticulously organised in beautiful rosewood drawers, every specimen labelled and dated in fine penmanship, every armoured back and helmeted, devil-pronged head shining like polished black onyx. The wife had believed the crusted little bastards carried the plague, and she'd refused to fuck her husband, had denied him the marital bed every night but the first when they were married, that one time enough for twin sons. She'd snatched the purse out of Wesley Lewis Jr's hands, the first price he'd offered.

'Berlin's a dog!'

People turned, looked at him, turned away again. He put his head down to rest on his arm; his other hand still held the mug. He slept, dreamless, until Mr Hendrik came to fetch him.

AN EASY DECISION

It was almost midnight when Krüger rushed downstairs from his room. He'd fallen asleep in his clothes and dreamed that he'd left his notebook on the table, but then woke and realised it was true.

Otto's coffee house was busy. He asked one of the serving girls but she had no idea, so Krüger went over to the table in the corner where he'd sat earlier.

A man there, his face shadowed by the lamps hanging low from the ceiling beams. He was spooning soup over a piece of bread that stood in the middle of his bowl. Another man too, asleep, stretched out along the bench, snoring. On the table was an empty bottle of schnapps and another bowl of soup.

The first man looked up and it was only now that Krüger noticed he was a Negro.

'Eat while it is hot,' the man said and resumed spooning the soup over his bread. He nodded at his snoring companion. 'He will never get to it.'

'I wanted to ask if you'd seen a notebook here, sir,' Krüger said. He held up his hands, palms facing, and made a width. 'About this size. I left it here earlier.'

Mr Hendrik shook his head. 'You sound hopeful. I am sorry. Was it important?'

Krüger sat down, defeated. 'Thoughts,' he said. 'Ideas.'

'Maybe it is for the best then.' The Negro pointed at the soup. 'Eat.'

The invitation seemed so normal and familiar that Krüger dragged the bowl over and picked up the spoon.

'Thank you,' he said, and began to tear at the bread that came with the soup, dropping the pieces into the bowl.

They introduced themselves, and after they'd eaten the soup they ordered mugs of beer. They asked polite questions of each other. Naturally, the talk turned to electrical eels.

'Can they kill a man?' Krüger said.

Mr Hendrik nodded. 'It is an unpleasant death.'

'How do you catch them?'

'There are different ways. The Indians use wild horses to drive them out of the mud, then push them into baskets with reeds.'

'What happens to the horses?'

'They panic and fall. Some are killed, some drown.'

Krüger sat back, wrists on the table edge. He tried to imagine it. At the same time, he suddenly fathomed just how truly vast the world was.

'You've come a long way,' he said. 'Collectors must pay handsomely.'

Mr Hendrik smiled. The whites of his eyes were yellowish in the lamplight of the inn.

'Power,' Krüger said. 'To own rarities.'

'They believe it exists in things.'

Krüger picked up his beer and drank. The ale was dark and strong and made him feel expanded. 'Sometimes believing is enough to make things true,' he said.

Wesley Lewis Jr mumbled in his sleep.

'In Surinam, the rebel slaves wear *obia* around their necks, for protection,' Mr Hendrik said. 'You would call them talismans. The rebel slaves believe muskets cannot harm them when they wear the *obia*. They charge the Dutch without fear. Of those who are shot dead, they say *he did not believe enough.*'

'Do you believe?'

Mr Hendrik opened his coat and undid two buttons on his shirt. He pulled out a corded necklace of coarse woven grass.

There was a knot tied into it, with a thick finger of carved bone through the middle, strange markings down its length.

'A gift from my sister,' he said.

Krüger saw scars across the man's chest, like lines of jagged candle wax. He stared at them, shocked at the silent violence they contained.

'You were a slave,' Krüger said.

'I am still a slave.'

Krüger looked at the sleeping man. 'Is he your master?'

Mr Hendrik shook his head. 'Not even of himself,' he said. 'My master is in Surinam.'

'He let you come?'

Mr Hendrik tucked the *obia* back inside his shirt, did up the buttons. 'He has my sister,' he said, and felt the longing for Josephine.

'So you'll go back.'

'Of course.'

'When?'

Mr Hendrik and Wesley Lewis Jr were due to leave for Rotterdam in the morning. The money for the electrical eels would be deposited at the master's bank there, and then a few days later they'd board the *Hoogendijk* and sail back to Paramaribo.

The two men ordered more beer and spoke of different things and sometimes sat through comfortable silences.

Back in his room, Krüger lay down on the bed. He sank heavily into the straw mattress and his head spun wildly. There's nothing for me in Berlin, he thought.

Without Hilde, there was nothing for him anywhere in dead, bloody Europe.

Why not Paramaribo? Why not?

A FAMILY AFFAIR

Captain Willem van der Velde stood in loose, cool, fine silk clothes, wearing a wide-brimmed hat against the glare, a long thin pipe in his hand which he smoked with quick puffs. His cheeks glowed, flushed with gin, his blue eyes squinting. He belched and swayed in the heat. Hamstringing was a standard punishment, but he always liked to supervise.

Beside him stood a young female slave, tray in hand with more supply of liquor. Her name was Anja. Her naked breasts were scratched and her bottom lip was swollen and bruised, the work of the master's wife that morning when she found Anja in the master's bed, a position she should have vacated before sunrise (these were the rules) but hadn't due to her inebriation. And now, like her master, she stood there beneath the torturous sun and fought the nauseous agitations of her body, trying desperately to hold the trembling tray straight. Her lip throbbed and sweat stung at the raw fingernail marks striping her breasts.

She put her mind in her toes. She concentrated on the mouldering dark green leaves and the rich moist soil; she squeezed it between her toes. She put her mind in her toes and didn't think about the boy being hamstrung, who was her son. And she didn't think about the butcher, who was her half-brother. And she didn't think about her belly, where a child by the master now grew.

Later, when the child was born, her half-brother's same knife was used to sever the cord. She named the master's child Josephine. By then her son had learned to walk again and Captain Willem van der Velde had Mr Hendrik help with raising the girl. His wife knew that he was the father and she regularly beat Mr Hendrik and his mother, and Josephine too, when she was old enough to be beaten, and this was just what life was like. The master had sired many children, but Josephine was beautiful from the beginning and only became more so as she grew, which was too much an affront to the master's wife (and their unattractive daughters), and as much a temptation to the father as any of the other slave girls on his plantation.

BOOK III

THE 4E RÉGIMENT ÉTRANGERS

Posen was damp, the wind was keen, the sky was an open window, bright blue with cold. Here, Johannes and Wolfie were officially enlisted into the ranks of the 4e Régiment Étrangers: three battalions or thereabouts, mostly Prussian prisoners of war and deserters, plus a mix of variously criminal Danes, Swedes and Russians. In other words, Grande Armée cannon fodder.

They'd marched from Berlin; their shoes were wrecked. 'And now we're a hundred 'n fifty miles closer to being blown up,' Wolfie said.

The first day was long and confused. The French shouted orders from their mounts, rode fast up and down the columns, their horses kicking divots of turf at the new recruits. From one endless line to the next, Johannes and Wolfie stood and waited, never quite knowing what they were waiting for. In one line, the rumour was food, boiled potatoes and *schinken*, but when they got to the front of the queue there was no *schinken* and the potatoes were only half cooked. In another line they were vaccinated for smallpox, the needle jabbed right through their sleeves by an old, unbuttoned orderly smoking a pipe and flanked by two grenadiers. (*'S'il vous plaît,'* he said in a monotone to every man, then, *'Je vous remercie.'*) Later, in the last line of the day, they were given uniforms: a green Prussian fusilier kollet with a red collar and white epaulettes, a white-plumed shako, green pants and red vest, hussar boots, white cross-belts and a brown leather knapsack, cartridge boxes, an infantry sword and scabbard, and a light musket of dubious condition (not that Johannes had any idea about muskets). Weighed down with their new uniforms and equipment, the men were then marched to a soggy green field on the outskirts of the city, where rows and rows of canvas tents marked a vast square alongside a riverbank. There were soldiers everywhere Johannes looked, standing in groups beside smoky braziers, muskets bayonet-racked in perfect spiky clusters around them, stern, empty looks upon their faces.

The chill off the fast-flowing river burned the men's cheeks. The crisp breeze swayed the grass and rustled the linden trees. The sound of the river, the wind, the earthy, wet green smell of the grass kindled childhood memories that made the men feel very far from home. All of this was in the air, a foreboding, of winter approaching, of hardship down the line.

'When do we run?' Johannes said. Wolfie had promised him they would.

'Soon,' Wolfie said. He could see the fear in the boy's eyes. He reached out and squeezed his shoulder. 'We'll be all right for now.'

LOVE IS REJECTION

Earlier in the year, a young Polish artist had come to paint Aunt Margaretha's portrait. His name was Kasimir Wieczorkowski and he'd recently been making a name for himself in Berlin. He was a serious young man, temperamental, and barely spoke to anybody in the house (he'd stayed in the room where the général was now lodged). Elisabeth von Hoffmann never saw him smile the whole time. Each day he woke late and waited for a platter of bread and cheese to be brought to his room, together with a bottle of warm beer (conditions of his accepting the commission), and then he spent a lot of time over his breakfast, almost until noon. Aunt Margaretha sat waiting for him in the study, where the light was deemed best, and looked at herself in the large mirror opposite her chair, at first practising and admiring her different poses, then slumped a little in the shoulders as she grew tired of waiting for Wieczorkowski to appear. Eventually, he would come out to work, though this didn't involve any actual painting. Mostly, at the start, he'd just sit there, staring at Aunt Margaretha, silent and brooding.

In fact, the artist didn't pick up a brush for a whole week. 'You don't know how to sit!' he'd say, tearing up the brief pencil sketch he'd made into the smallest pieces he could manage.

Rather than paint, he fussed for hours over the way Margaretha von Hoffmann sat. He adjusted her head, her arms, her shoulders, the folding of her hands in her lap, the folds of her skirts. He snapped at her in Polish if she moved. Elisabeth was shocked by how her aunt bore his insolence, and expected any day for the artist to be thrown out into the street by Günther. But vanity has terrific qualities of endurance.

And then, at last, during the second week of his residence, he began to paint.

Kasimir Wieczorkowski's hair was long and the colour of wheat and he constantly flicked it out of his eyes with a quick movement of his head. He had long slender fingers, a fine straight nose and blue-grey eyes that were, if one were truthful, probably a little too close together. He was thin, his clothes hung loose on his frame, and his paleness must have been from all the cheese he ate.

Elisabeth von Hoffmann told her friends about Kasimir, though her version was far more flattering.

She entered his room one night (barefoot, her toes like ice) and closed the door carefully behind her. There was a brief metallic *clack* of the lock as she turned the key, and then she heard Kasimir sit up in bed. Elisabeth went over quickly, heart beating, breathless and yet relieved. She'd reached the peak of her courage and would now relinquish the event to the artist. He'd know what to do next.

In the dark, the bed creaked, the mattress bounced, blankets ruffled. She slipped in and lay down, the soft pillows billowing up around her ears (she felt his warmth in them, smelled his hair). Her excitement was intense, her skin alive. She closed her eyes and waited for the touch of his elegant hands.

But instead there was the sound of limbs sliding between the sheets, and again the intense creaking and bouncing of the bed. Breathing. Whispering? Then nothing.

Elisabeth said, 'Kasimir?'

In a weak, croaky voice, the artist, who must have been standing beside the bed now, said, 'Please go away.'

Elisabeth's eyes adapted to the dark. There was a silhouette standing beside the bed, framed by the curtained window. Kasimir, obviously: but no. There were *two* silhouettes.

Again, the artist, in a whisper now, but firmly: '*Please. You must go.*'

The other silhouette cleared its throat.

Elisabeth went back to her room. The next day, the artist Kasimir Wieczorkowski ignored her completely. As did the family lawyer, Seidlitz.

THE INTERPRETATION OF DREAMS

In late December, Grande Armée in tow, Bonaparte sped from Berlin in his carriage, first to Posen, then to Warsaw, en route to Russia. Along the way, he met an eighteen-year-old Polish countess named Marie Walewska.

It was a coincidental first meeting, on a snowy New Year's Eve. Bonaparte's carriage was welcomed on the outskirts of Warsaw by a crowd of Polish nationalists, among whom was the fetching young countess in her red-amber fox fur hat. Fair and beautiful (and married to an old count), she was granted permission to approach the carriage, where she handed the Emperor a bouquet of flowers and so caught his wandering eye. Some historians argue this story was a romantic fabrication and that it was in fact Talleyrand who'd plucked her from his 'pockets full of girls' (Bonaparte's own words) and delivered the young countess to Napoleon's attentions, but no matter; the result remains the same.

The Emperor slept warmly during his brief Polish sojourn.

Countess Walewska moved into the Schloss Finckenstein (Bonaparte's temporary headquarters) and nobody there could quite work the demure little countess out. She didn't play cards, she didn't drink or giggle or raise her voice, and she hid her voluptuous, pale Polish curves beneath unflattering clothes. Marie Walewska was not typical of Bonaparte's lovers, and yet . . . and yet.

Her devotion and love for the Emperor grew fierce as his own fresh passion fired and burned during those winter weeks. But what would happen, what would eventuate . . . well, this was in hands other than her own.

True love relinquished all control.

The Empress Josephine, meanwhile, had been begging to join Bonaparte, sending numerous insisting letters. *I am so miserable without you*, she wrote, *and always in tears.* The balance of their love had shifted since the coronation and the change in Napoleon worried her deeply. She couldn't give him a son. She would be abandoned, discarded, just like one of his many lovers. Her hand trembled over the pages, new letters begun as soon as the previous ones were sealed and sent.

I cannot breathe with you so far away. You must send for me.

From Warsaw, Bonaparte wrote: *This is no time of year to travel. It is cold and the roads are bad and unsafe. So I cannot allow you to undertake so many trials and dangers.*

Josephine was no fool but she suffered the rejection with less than her usual grace. One terrible night she even dreamed of the bouquet, of which she knew (as she knew of the young Countess Walewska and most everything else that involved her husband on campaign). In her dream she saw the bouquet on the carriage seat beside Napoleon who, as the horses began to pull away, tossed the flowers through the window and left them fallen on the snow, forgotten. In the dream, Josephine couldn't tell what kind of flowers they were and was desperate to see, to know, as though this might dispel her distress, but the distance grew and the snow became silvered, then dark, and everything became strange and distorted, as so often happens in dreams. She woke and threw the covers off in a panic, felt she was suffocating beneath them. Later, after she left Mainz and returned to France, not even her magnificent gardens at Malmaison were able to ease her sense of dread.

The Countess Walewska might have feared worse, had she endured such a dream, for it was in fact her own bouquet that was tossed from the carriage window. And, indeed, the dream would have proven prophetic; months later and pregnant with the Emperor's illegitimate son, she waited in vain for Bonaparte to send for her in Warsaw, while instead he set about in earnest search of a worthy wife among the royal families of Europe. But neither the Countess Walewska nor the Empress Josephine could really claim the dream. In truth, the dream was Napoleon's. It was he who'd conquered their sleep.

HIGHWAY ROBBERY

There was the carriage driver and Mr Hendrik, Wesley Lewis Jr and the Prussian, Krüger, who'd come along at the last.

They got to Oschersleben easily enough, but a few miles short of Wolfenbüttel (it was dusk, foggy) they were held up by bandits.

Four men with pistols rode out of the trees and surrounded the carriage. The chestnut gelding and the mottled grey mare reared and sent everyone inside lunging suddenly forwards and then backwards. They were summoned from the carriage and directed to kneel on the ground.

'Move swiftly,' one of the bandits said, pointing his pistol. A red kerchief hid his face (the others wore kerchiefs in different colours). He remained on his horse while his colleagues dismounted and patted down the prisoners for wallets, weapons and blades. They found nothing but the driver's apple knife and his sad little pigskin of small silver and coppers (they completely missed Mr Hendrik's knife, the sheath tucked up in his armpit). Then they climbed up onto the carriage and threw the luggage down from the roof, opened the trunks and tore through the bags and spilled everything over the ground. They unhitched the two horses as well and led them away.

Wesley Lewis Jr watched as one of the bandits used the hilt of his sword to break the lid of the smallest chest. It had been under the seat in the carriage with them. The bandit tore the splintered wood away and tipped everything upside down. It was the chest with the false bottom, where Mr Hendrik had hidden their travel money for the way over and now the money for the electrical eels, all of Claus von Rolt's beautiful shiny gold coins. Captain van der Velde had given it to them at the start of the journey, showed them how it worked. The false bottom came away as the bandit cracked the chest against the ground, but he didn't notice; and, anyway, there were no gold coins in there. He threw the shattered timbers away, went to work on another of the trunks.

Where was the goddamn money? Wesley Lewis Jr turned to Mr Hendrik. 'You black son of a bitch.'

The man on the horse said, 'Shut it!'

Afterwards, when the thieves had ridden away, a light rain began to fall. Krüger stood up and helped Mr Hendrik to his feet. The driver brushed the grass and dirt from his knees and swore. They were still miles from the next waylaying inn, and now they were horseless and stuck.

Wesley Lewis Jr watched Mr Hendrik. He waited for him to say something, but the Negro wouldn't even look at him.

Finally, Wesley Lewis Jr said, 'So where is it?'

Mr Hendrik began to pick up some of their things from the ground. He had to stick his lame leg out a little to the side, stiffly, each time he bent down.

'You'll not tell me?'

'It's safe,' Mr Hendrik said.

The rain was still only a faint drizzle, but the clouds had darkened. The cool mist was sweet with the smell of trees, and rich, luxuriant soil.

'You son of a bitch,' Wesley Lewis Jr said again. 'What if something happens to your black carcass? What then? I'm out with the beggars?'

Mr Hendrik ignored him.

'We'll have to spend the night,' the driver said, draping a coat over his shoulders. 'Unless somebody comes along and finds us.'

Wesley Lewis Jr stood there, didn't move, didn't speak, anger swelling in his chest and squeezing his throat.

'I'll try for the next village in the morning,' the driver said.

Wesley Lewis Jr booted one of the empty trunks across the grass.

When the rain started properly, they sat in the carriage and listened to it pummel the roof. The floor inside was wet and muddy, and there were places where the carriage leaked and the water trickled down onto the seats and everybody had to sit slightly forward. Krüger balanced a few books on his lap, wiping them clean with a rag. One of the bandit's horses had trampled them into the ground.

There was *Kritik der reinen Vernunft* and *Maria Stuart* and *Wilhelm Meisters Lehrjahre*. There was Hilde's copy of *Hyperion; oder, Der Eremit in Griechenland*, too, and he also had Mr Hendrik's Bible in his lap, a leather-bound copy in Dutch that Captain Willem van der Velde had given him for the journey ('So they won't think you're a dirty black heathen,' he'd said).

The rain drummed the carriage and it was cold now and getting darker and each man had a blanket over his shoulders.

Wesley Lewis Jr pointed at the books in Krüger's lap. 'If we had a candle, you could read us all a fucking bedtime story.'

LOVE IS UNPREDICTABLE

Général Fourés thought about Elisabeth von Hoffmann all the time. He thought about her in the morning and throughout the afternoon, and of course he thought about her at night, too. He played out in his mind any number of fantastic scenes between them, erotic and banal, though mainly erotic. He was exasperated, living under the same roof, and yet thrilled at the same time, because he could see her so often and without contriving to. The tensions of propriety (there had been none in his seduction of Letizia) were providing an unexpected satisfaction.

Elisabeth was short-tempered with him, especially if Günther was around. But, as the days passed, their brief interactions grew longer. She'd ask him a question or two now, just simple things, yet their conversations gradually took up a little extra time and so the moments between them lingered, acquired space. She still frequently bruised his brightness with her youthful, contemptuous dismissals of him (that look!), but soon it was done with a solicitous smile, brief, casual, intimate because it was almost unnoticeable, though the général noticed. He noticed everything to do with Elisabeth von Hoffmann, the smallest detail and slightest change in the air.

Except of course the night she came into his room and slipped into the bed and grabbed his hand and put it to her breast. All day, all week, he hadn't noticed a thing that might have predicted the occasion.

She'd squirmed up against him, gathered his feet in hers. She'd said, 'You know what to do, Général, don't you?'

OBJETS D'HISTOIRE

Claus von Rolt held the square of bloodstained cloth in the palm of his hand. There was a vague swirl to the pattern, yellowish where it thinned out to the edges of the fraying material, and a rich red brown everywhere else. It looked like nothing, like a patch that had been used to dress a wound maybe, and Rolt was mildly repulsed by it, thinking of pain and blood, the stink of bandages. He held it up closer to his nose, expecting something pungent, but detected only a vague mustiness, and the slightly sweated odour of cold bedsheets. He touched a corner of the cloth with the tip of his little finger and couldn't help but marvel at how close he was to history.

It was exactly things like this that thrilled him.

'What do you think?' Christophe Bergerard asked.

'There's the question of authenticity,' Rolt said.

Général Fourés's aide-de-camp carefully took the piece of cloth from Rolt's palm and placed it back inside a small, velvet-lined box. 'I assure you, sir,' he said, 'the article is genuine.'

Rolt smiled. 'Yes, well, you may say it . . .'

Christophe Bergerard had been given Rolt's name by his father, who'd heard it from a London taxidermist and dealer in rare species. Now, in Berlin with Général Fourés, Bergerard had sought the Prussian out. He was a young man with a tendency to live beyond his means, a tendency often requiring redress.

'I do not part with it lightly,' he said, frowning at Claus von Rolt. 'And even now question myself.'

The cloth in its special box had been a gift from his father, a good luck charm. The blood of the guillotined queen, Marie Antoinette, soaked up in a fishmonger's apron, right off the cobblestones of the place de la Révolution, moments after her head had rolled into the basket and the blood had surged from her severed neck. Not having enjoyed much luck since it had come into his possession, Christophe Bergerard thought it was about time for Queen Marie to deliver.

'My father was there,' Bergerard said. 'He saw the sun glint off the poised blade, he saw the Queen's elegant neck placed in the choke, and then the blade's sudden, swift descent. *Pffft!* He heard the roar of the crowd as her head fell into the basket and saw the blood flow in torrents, down off the boards and over the ground. And then the filthy peasants all ran up with their aprons and dresses and shirts and sheets, fought each other and wrestled in the blood, kneeled and sopped it all up in a frenzy, like animals.'

Rolt wondered how many times the boy had told his father's story.

'The filthy rabble,' Christophe Bergerard said. He opened the box again, allowed Rolt a second look at the cloth. It was all true, every detail. His father had been among the crowd and then followed one of the women who'd brought her linen bundles with her for the soaking up. They'd been at it all week with the lesser aristocrats, but the Queen's blood was the prize that day and the rush to the foot of the guillotine was as intense as any charge of dragoons.

'Her name was Madame Sulzer and she was a fishmonger's wife,' Bergerard said. 'She refused to sell my father the whole apron. Only this one portion.'

'A shrewd businesswoman,' Rolt said.

'You need not doubt its authenticity.'

What I don't doubt, Claus von Rolt thought to himself, is the power of the idea. He might even keep the piece for himself.

He made a generous offer and the happy young French aide-de-camp accepted.

DRUM

Training.

Johannes Meyer fired the musket and again completely missed the target. He'd also tamped too much powder down the barrel and almost blown his own head off. His cheek was hot and blackened from the exploding flintlock and his ears were ringing painfully. He dropped the musket to the ground. For the moment, the whole world was a giant tuning fork.

The sergeant instructor was yelling at him, but Johannes had his back turned and couldn't hear a thing. Furious, the man began to stride over, whacking a long cane against his boots as he walked. The two soldiers on either side of Johannes backed away. Wolfie, further along the line and seeing what was happening, stepped out and stood to attention as the sergeant approached, hoping to distract him with a question, but the sergeant just pushed him roughly aside. Johannes, his hands clasped to his ears, turned to see the sergeant instructor suddenly right there in front of him. In the next instant, the sergeant's cane went up and Johannes went to his knees, ears still ringing and now fresh pain exploding through his shoulder.

'Get up!' the sergeant instructor said. He'd hit Johannes so hard the cane had snapped in two and fractured the boy's collarbone. 'On your feet!'

Just then three horses galloped down the line of men: a French officer, flanked by two aides-de-camp. When they were level with the sergeant, the officer reined his horse hard and the animal whinnied and spun around, a huge chestnut stallion with black legs and a white blaze. The aides-de-camp pulled their animals up too, churning up the ground, and now all the men with their muskets could see the officer was a colonel-en-second, his plumed shako with a gold-braided chinstrap, his blue pelisse intensely buttoned, a dolman cape over his shoulder. Large silver spurs shone immaculately on his black hussar boots.

'What's going on here?' he said. 'What has this man done?'

The sergeant instructor stood to attention. 'He is incapable of firing a musket, Colonel.'

'Since when has it been taught with a cane, Sergeant?' The colonel-en-second's name was Josse-Fridolin-Jacques-Antoine-Félix-Séraphin-Stanislas de Freuler. He despised the barbaric Prussian disciplinary methods and had opposed the practice being maintained in the Grande Armée, but the Emperor had been convinced to allow his foreign regiments to keep their traditions.

'I believe he is purposely refusing to obey simple instructions, Colonel,' the sergeant said. He was a brute (that much was obvious), short and gnarled, with phlegmy grey eyes.

The colonel-en-second looked down at Johannes, crumpled and holding his shoulder, unable to stand up. For a moment he thought to spur his horse on, leave the matter alone. There was so much else to do today, tomorrow, and all the days following. But he turned to one of the aides-de-camp on his left. He'd had an idea and, when they came unbidden like that, he always regarded them as gifts. They had never denied him pleasure and reward, as he'd never failed to act upon them.

'Have this man attended to,' he said, pointing at Johannes. 'And bring him to me in the morning.'

'Yes, Colonel.'

'He's to be our new regiment drummer. Understood?'

'Yes, Colonel.'

Colonel-en-second Freuler swung his horse around and galloped away, pleased with himself and his magnanimity.

RESOLUTIONS

In the morning, the oak trees were dark with rain and shrouded in mist. The birdcalls were soft, tentative, the world still and contained, like a church.

One by one, they stepped out of the carriage, weary and silent, only the creak of springs to disturb the quiet, as the carriage leaned in and out of the shifting weight.

The driver wanted to head immediately for the next village to notify the authorities and hire fresh horses.

'Some apples and walnuts,' he said, handing over a bucket that he kept for his now-stolen team. Then he took two or three quick pulls on the bottle of brandy he kept under the seat for himself. 'I'll leave you this, too.'

'You're a kind man,' Wesley Lewis Jr said, taking the bottle.

'Well, hopefully I won't be too long.'

'Shouldn't we all go?' Krüger said. 'Together?'

'I'm not walking anywhere,' Wesley Lewis Jr said. 'And Mr Hendrik's got his lovely limp to contend with.'

The carriage driver said, 'There's no need. And I'd appreciate an eye on the carriage.'

It had been an uncomfortable night and they'd been robbed and his horses were gone, but as the driver cut through the woods to reach the road, there was some sense of relief. He was glad to leave the strange trio of men behind.

They stood around the carriage eating the apples and cracking walnuts.

'How long do you think he'll take?' Krüger said.

Mr Hendrik shrugged.

'Years,' Wesley Lewis Jr said and threw his half-eaten apple into the trees. Then he took the bottle of brandy up into the driver's seat and stretched out across it, an arm behind his head. 'Wake me up when he gets back.'

Mr Hendrik and Krüger cracked more walnuts and looked out into the trees.

Nobody spoke and each man drifted into his thoughts. Krüger saw Hilde, Mr Hendrik his sister. Wesley Lewis Jr swigged at the brandy with his eyes closed and resumed his contempt for everyone and everything, particularly the Negro.

Slowly the mist burned off and the sun rose bright and glassy, making the dew-beaded leaves glisten and sparkle. Krüger decided to take a walk through the oak grove. Mr Hendrik, feeling the stiffness in his leg and wanting to lie down, took a blanket and spread it over the ground in a patch of sunshine not far from the carriage. He stretched out on his back, put Captain van der Velde's Bible under his head and stared up into the sky. Soon his eyes grew heavy and he fell asleep.

When he heard Mr Hendrik begin to snore, Wesley Lewis Jr climbed down from the driver's seat and searched through everything the bandits had left behind. But there were no false bottoms in the other trunks, no secret compartments. He looked through the clothes, felt every pocket and squeezed every lining, collar, hem and sleeve, turned everything inside out, but there was nothing there either. Nothing anywhere.

He sat in the carriage and watched Mr Hendrik through the open door. The Negro's got the money on him somewhere, he thought. He must have. Son of a bitch.

Wesley Lewis Jr worked at the bottle. Mr Hendrik slept. The ground steamed a little in the sun, warm as fresh dung.

In life, it was important to determine goals and hold to them, if you were ever to taste success. He remembered how his father used to say, 'You think Jesus Christ Our Lord and Saviour didn't know exactly what he was doing?'

Well, Wesley Lewis Jr thought, I know exactly what *I'm* going to do.

I'm going to kill the Negro.

I'm going to take Captain van der Velde's money.

I'm going to sail back to Paramaribo and find Josephine and take her away and fuck her forever.

No more hunting and trading animal hides, no more sweating through forests, no more goddamn mosquitoes. And no more Mr Hendrik.

Wesley Lewis Jr tipped the bottle to his lips and drank to his new resolution.

LOVE IS REVOLUTION

Général Fourés fell quickly in love, of course. At his age, these were miracles and not to be denied their due and devotion.

After the first shocking, phenomenal, impossible occasion, the young Prussian beauty visited him every night she could, which was most nights (the von Hoffmann house was full of old people who slept and dreamed like the dead, never stirring until the morning) and in the golden candlelight and beneath the warmth of goose-down quilts, in the thrall of her sweet-scented skin and smooth heat and willing youth, the sound of her pleasure, her naked breath in his ear, he was a lion. Insatiable and born again in love, a creature fully possessed of itself. He was beyond the intoxications of wine, it had no power over him: Fourés could consume oceans now and balance a sword on the tip of his tongue. He was cured and immune to common men, their misdirections and illusions, to common ailments, to fear, to frost, the beating sun; his joints were supple, his muscles lean and strong, his stomach an iron drum no food could defeat. Kings' sons did not have what he had, not his own sons. He had everything, the world, distilled through loops of copper and a thousand years contained in each drop, just one under the tongue enough for a lifetime, and the général with a cellar full of barrels.

DRUMMER BOYS ARE LOVED

The drum was battered and scratched, fringed in black-and-gold bands and a few thin tassels still hanging by a thread. The calfskin was brittle, yellow, the white leather straps worn and stained. There was a bullet hole in the brass shell too, entry and opposite exit, both now stopped with cork and patched with gum and leather. The drum had been captured from an Austrian regiment during the Battle of Austerlitz, and it was how the Austrian drummer boy had died, shot through the brass and then bled to death, an artery severed in his groin. Some of his dried blood was still in the tassels.

The corporal said, 'Christ, try it again.'

There was much to learn: the March, the Quickstep, the Charge. There were coded beats encompassing orders to move formations across the battlefield (played from drummer to drummer, down the hill from where the maréchals watched, mounted, beside the Emperor), and tunes that made the men laugh, whether to ease the prelude to battle or lighten the epilogues of blood and loss. Everything had to be snapped out crisp and clear, resounding. Ears, hands, heart, mind, legs simultaneously stepping across the cannoned terrain, the body in perfect, cold balance. It was vital not to cock it up.

The corporal said, 'Stop cocking it up!'

The 4e Régiment Étrangers was marching out soon and Johannes Meyer didn't have a lot of time left in which to learn.

Behind him, in a huddle, the grimy fifer boys watched.

'Who gave him the drum?'

'Some fool.'

'He's too old!'

'Too tall!'

'The snipers will pick him out easy.'

'He'll get his head blown off for sure.'

The drum was luck, you see, a talisman of hope, the regiment's beating heart, not to be lost. It marked the safe path through the blinding smoke and fire of battle. The boys who drummed were loved and tossed coins the soldiers had kissed and muttered quick prayers over. The drummer boys were loved like favourite nephews, and looked like them too, for every man, eventually.

The drummer boys were fragrant yellow apples!

The fifers kept their voices low, out of misfortune's ear, lest they made things worse than they already were.

'We're all done for.'

'Shut up!'

'Better it's said.'

'Then say it somewhere else.'

'Too late!'

'Arsehole!'

Nobody liked the look of Johannes Meyer.

THE WORLD THROUGH A TUNNEL

The carriage driver still hadn't returned and neither had the Prussian.

Wesley Lewis Jr was covering the distance (action! poise!). He restrained his stride and placed his feet carefully. There was a length of oak in his right hand, a branch about the size of an axe handle, thick and hefted. He'd picked it clean of leaves and loose bark. It was a terrific piece of wood.

The sun was high now. It was a crisp, beautiful day. Mr Hendrik was still asleep.

Wesley Lewis Jr was sweating and his mouth was dry.

CAPTAIN VAN DER VELDE'S BIBLE

Captain van der Velde had inherited the Bible from his wife's first husband, who'd brought it to Paramaribo from Holland.

It had been specially crafted for him by a bookbinder in Antwerp. The leather-bound boards had been made thicker than usual, and the bookbinder had cut a cavity into the boards, creating a sleeve beneath the endpapers.

'Nobody ever steals a Bible,' the first husband had explained to his wife. 'It will protect our stake better than any iron box under lock and key.'

In one sleeve alone, there were enough flat, lozenge-shaped gold ingots to purchase an abundance of land, slaves, barges and connections in Paramaribo.

Captain van der Velde liked to read to the slaves from this clever holy book, but a few days before Wesley Lewis Jr and Mr Hendrik departed for Europe with the barrel of electrical eels, he'd called Mr Hendrik into his study and shown him the hidden sleeves beneath the endpapers.

'The American needn't know.'

And he still didn't know, though Wesley Lewis Jr was much closer, closer than he'd ever been. He stood over Mr Hendrik and watched him for a moment, asleep, his head resting on the Bible. Then he tapped the Negro's lame leg with the oak bough in his hand.

'My daddy used to say *bad dreams at night when you doze in the day*,' he said. 'So time to get up now.'

Mr Hendrik blinked at the sun flashing over the American's shoulder. It made a bright haze around his head.

'Up now, sweetness.' Wesley Lewis Jr laughed. 'Plenty of time for sleeping when we're dead!'

Mr Hendrik saw the length of wood in the American's hand. He frowned and began to lift his head, tucked his elbows in close to his body in the effort to get up.

'On second thoughts . . .'

Wesley Lewis Jr put a boot to Mr Hendrik's chest and pushed him back flat. He swung the length of wood up high and then grunted and brought it down as hard as he could on the Negro's hamstrung leg.

DEBUT

The sound of it, the way Wolfie bit into the sausage, the way the skin around it popped in his teeth and then the chewing with his mouth open, all of it turned Johannes Meyer's stomach.

'Eat something,' Wolfie said. 'It'll do you good.'

Johannes looked away. They'd left Posen and marched across eastern Prussia and then they'd marched across Poland. Endless days, endless weeks of marching. Along the way, Johannes had practised and practised, the March, the Quickstep, the Charge, but the fifer boys still kept their distance.

There was the boom of cannon fire all around and the drum rattled beside him on the ground.

'They said he came through the night before,' Wolfie said, meaning Bonaparte. He was trying to distract the boy, get him talking and not thinking about the battle. He bit into the sausage again, spoke with his mouth full. 'Wonder if we'll see him?'

'I have to go,' Johannes said and picked up the drum.

'See you for breakfast, boy,' Wolfie said after him. 'We'll have us some good Russian *kolbasa!*'

Johannes smiled nervously, nodded, and walked off. He went in search of the fifers but couldn't find them anywhere.

The Battle of Heilsberg began that night, at ten o'clock. Johannes drummed the orders, standing on a hill not far from a line of officers, all of them mounted on jittery horses, boots shiny black and silver-spurred, reins in gloved hands. They said Bonaparte was on the next hill along. The Emperor spoke through Johannes's hands, in rolls and raps and *rat-a-tat-tats*.

The sky flashed with cannon fire, the ground rumbled, shards of iron exploded through the flaring darkness. Infantry and cavalry clashed. Within an hour, the brave but headstrong Maréchal Jean Lannes, Duc de Montebello (who should have waited and held the attack but simply couldn't restrain himself) lost over two thousand of his men. The battle ended by petering out, a mess of bodies and horses, each side exhausted and without honour, flaying blindly through the morning, until the Russians retreated and the French gave chase.

Four days later, as dusk fell, Colonel-en-second Freuler said, 'Forward!', and this time Johannes Meyer wasn't up on a hill but inside the turmoil on the ground. He hit the drum and began to walk (his legs shaking uncontrollably) and a battalion of the 4e Régiment Étrangers followed him into the Battle of Friedland.

Within seconds of starting the Quickstep, the battle had swallowed them whole, like a huge, grinding, red-bloody mouth.

There were soldiers everywhere, dead, crawling, running, limbless, gutted, thousands of soldiers. The cannons thundered.

'Keep moving! Forward!'

He wasn't a coward, but the world was being torn apart, its heart ripped out. It was just like Goethe's story of the island with its magnetic mountain and the ships that sailed too close, all the iron torn from their timbers, nails and bolts and braces, and the ships collapsed and broke apart, the sailors killed by falling spars and yards. The battle was a force all its own and drew everything into its centre, grinding relentlessly through the thirty thousand men who eventually lay dead and injured.

The impossible noise, the soldiers everywhere, the drum at Johannes's hip, smacking his leg as he marched and drummed, onwards, or was it in circles, who could tell?

And then he was running.

It was as though his body had willed it and not his mind, running, and the drum like a man at his leg, trying to pull him down, and Johannes panicked and ran as hard as he could, he'd never run so fast.

Maybe he was a coward.

The air burned his lungs and ahead of him were more soldiers, soldiers, soldiers, French or Russian he couldn't tell, and they cried out and died and were torn by explosions, and then up ahead he saw the shadowed darkness of trees and they were very still and quiet and nobody called out and nobody shot him and the trees were there, a miracle. Johannes Meyer almost wept at the sight of the trees, they were so close, and he was running towards them and he couldn't believe the trees, and then suddenly he was there, inside the trees, he was there, and he believed them.

BOOK IV

THE NEGER VRIJCORPS

In Surinam, Captain Willem van der Velde was something of a hero.

Back in 1772 he'd successfully led his free Negroes (the Black Rangers) against the rebel runaway slaves known as the Bonis, who, emboldened by greater numbers, hunger and revenge, had attacked the white plantations, murdered the masters and their families, and plundered the bursting store-houses. In time, they'd reached the very outskirts of the capital Paramaribo, forcing the gouty lords of sugar to take action. Unfit to fight the Bonis themselves (the thought of it amused their wives), they decided to buy an army.

'But the cheapest going,' they all agreed. 'We have expenses!'

The masters pooled a woeful purse and secured a beggarly regiment of freed slaves and former soldiers with gruesome, mercenary résumés. One of them was Captain Willem van der Velde: originally from Haarlem, barely a year in the colony and looking for any opportunity.

He quickly acquired a reputation for ruthlessness, and proved an innovative and creative dispenser of summary justice (the masters approved enthusiastically). A favourite method was to stake captured rebels to the ground, have their legs and arms crushed with an iron bar, then wait for the fire ants to swarm out of their giant breasted hillocks and bite the runaway slave to death.

'Just chew,' he'd said to September, an Ouca Negro from Jocka Creek, as the ants crawled into his mouth and nose and ears, filled his eyes, the man writhing and screaming. 'I'll bring you a good claret.'

One day, when the Bonis attacked the Nederpelt plantation on the River Cottica, the captain met his future wife.

Katrijn Nederpelt watched the handsome and healthy Captain Willem van der Velde stride towards the house. His Black Rangers had chased the raiding Bonis into the forest and slaughtered them to a man, and she'd thanked God for His great and infinite benevolence. The previous year, in a drunken stupor, her husband, Hansie Hendrik Nederpelt, had fallen into the river and drowned. Maybe he was pushed (there were rumours). Regardless, she'd overseen the plantation ever since, though this was no place for a woman to be alone, and certainly not for one still so full of desires. Katrijn Nederpelt was a woman in her prime, and wasn't the only one who thought so. Alas, choices were few among the Dutchmen of Surinam, who expired like flies in the heat and debauchery. But the captain, well, obviously, here was someone special.

She invited Captain van der Velde to join her for a drink that evening, to celebrate his victory against the Bonis, in the cool shade of her deep verandah.

The Black Rangers busied themselves with hanging their haul of severed rebel hands on a rope stretched between two tamarind trees, then setting fires beneath to smoke and dry them. Each smoked hand was worth twenty-five florins back in Paramaribo and they'd gathered a prize collection, one of their best of recent months. Their mood was exuberant. Katrijn Nederpelt, not usually generous, had gifted them a few barrels of Kill-Devil rum. 'With thanks,' she'd said to Captain van der Velde, 'for your brave efforts.'

He removed his hat and stepped up into the shade of the verandah. She saw that his hair was rusty blond and his teeth gleamed like old porcelain.

'Please, Captain. Sit.'

Captain Willem van der Velde took the offered chair. She was older by a good five or six years he thought, but fair and plump and there was an authority in her manner that he liked. He already knew she was one of the richest women in the colony.

Katrijn Nederpelt indicated the small table between them, glasses and a bottle standing on a silver tray. 'Help yourself, Captain.'

'Thank you, Madame Nederpelt.' He poured them both gin, then toasted her. 'To your hospitality and health.'

'God willing.'

A slave girl came onto the verandah, carrying a white silk shirt.

'Anja will wash and repair your clothes, Captain,' Katrijn said. 'In the meantime, you may wear one of my late husband's shirts.'

'That is most kind of you.'

'Give yours to Anja now.'

The captain hesitated but then stood up, and Katrijn Nederpelt watched as he removed his shirt and handed it to the slave girl. He slipped her deceased husband's luxurious silk over his head. There was a faint aroma of cloves.

Van der Velde sat down again. Katrijn said, 'Anja, help the captain with his boots.'

The slave girl draped the soiled shirt on the verandah railing, then came over and turned her backside towards the captain and straddled his leg. She reached down to take up his boot (it was how she used to do it for Master Nederpelt), gripped the toes and behind the ankle and began to tug, eventually pulling the boot free. She did the same on the other leg.

Katrijn Nederpelt said, 'Go and clean them, girl. And don't forget the shirt.' She watched Anja go and smiled at Captain van der Velde. She felt there was some possibility they might understand one another. His eyes followed the slave girl. Yes, she thought so.

A young Negro boy came onto the verandah carrying a tray of fruit and smoked meats. He was dressed like a Dutch schoolboy, though barefoot.

'Captain,' Katrijn Nederpelt said, 'this is Mr Hendrik. He is my best man here.'

Mr Hendrik bowed.

'He will assist you with whatever you may need during your stay.'

Willem van der Velde smiled and nodded. 'You are spoiling me, Madame Nederpelt. I am not used to such luxuries.'

'Then you must apply yourself, Captain,' Katrijn Nederpelt said. 'And learn quickly.'

That night, she delivered Anja to the captain's room herself, and then sat down in a chair by the door to watch.

ORDERS

It wasn't until Elisabeth von Hoffmann was actually in the carriage and speeding away that the reality of what was happening settled on her and became true. After the initial joy of lightness, of unshackling, of freedom, there was a sudden moment of fear and doubt. She'd stiffened with the keen surprise of it, her heart beating. The brilliant lightness of escape had instantly plummeted, had weighed down without warning (she'd felt it physically in her body and pressed the heels of her palms into the carriage seat to brace herself). And then, as quickly as the fear had come, it was gone, dissolved. The moment passed.

Such doubts were naturally only ever fleeting in the young.

She turned to the général, put her head on his shoulder, and gazed out of the carriage window again. Dark and gloomy Berlin went by. Elisabeth was happier than she'd ever been in her life.

She had left a note for her aunt Margaretha on the side table in the hallway.

The général is to be the new governor in Cayenne and I am going with him. Forgive me, Aunt. And wish me well! Your Loving Niece . . .

Their plan had been hastily put together and they were giddy with it, the pleasure of its pending expressed in irrepressible smiles, even as they whispered and dressed and moved silently through the sleeping rooms that morning. Bergerard had already taken care of their luggage. They would ride for Paris and stay at the général's house in rue de la Chaussée-d'Antin for a fortnight while he completed various duties (and, though he feared the encounter, dealt with his wife). They'd then travel to Bordeaux and board a ship bound for the French colony of Guyane, in far-off South America.

In the coach, Général Fourés reached over and squeezed Elisabeth's hand. She turned her blossoming, youthful face towards him. The général felt like a young man eloping. Years fell away and the thrill was bright through his flesh, his bones.

The horses' hooves clattered on the road like iron drum rolls. He hadn't told Elisabeth that his new posting was a demotion, but right now, by God, what the hell did that matter?

A WALK IN THE WOODS

The way it happened: Krüger, returning from his walk, came through the trees and saw Wesley Lewis Jr in the clearing before the carriage. The American appeared to be kneeling on the ground and bent over. Krüger's mind took the image in lazily (had the American found something on the ground? Was he praying?) but within a few more steps he knew there was something unaccountable in it.

Then Krüger began to run.

He crashed into Wesley Lewis Jr, locking arms around the man's shoulders and pulling him to the ground, ended up with the American writhing on top of him, furious and yelling. Then Mr Hendrik, half strangled, gasping, rolled over and, before Krüger knew what was happening (he was still pinned under the American), Mr Hendrik thrust a knife into Wesley Lewis Jr's chest. Then he pulled it out and stabbed the American again, right through the ribs and into his heart.

Wesley Lewis Jr choked on the blood filling his throat (his eyes were wide, horrified, there was a thick, liquid sound coming from him) and then the colour in his face drained away and, a few moments after that, everything in his body stopped and he was dead.

Krüger felt the weight of the man pressing down on him. He breathed heavily and then realised his hands were wet, something warm, and when he brought his right hand up and saw it was blood, he pushed Wesley Lewis Jr off in a panic and rushed to his feet.

'My God!'

With his leg broken, Mr Hendrik couldn't move and groaned quietly with the pain, lying beside the dead American. Krüger tried to fathom what had happened. It was tremendous, unbelievable. A maelstrom of incomprehension.

THE COMTESSE D'ANJOU AND THE GIRL FROM ANGOULÊME

After peace was brokered and signed with the Russians (on a ridiculous canopied raft to which the Emperor and the Tsar were rowed on the river at Tilsit, in early July 1807), the Emperor returned to Paris to discover the Portuguese had changed their minds and their allegiances and were flirting with the English once again. In truth, they'd never stopped flirting, but now it was out in the open, and right in the Emperor's face too, and that just wouldn't do. So Bonaparte sent Général Jean-Andoche Junot and about twenty-five thousand men down to the Iberian Peninsula to sort the Portuguese out. Johannes Meyer and the 4e Régiment Étrangers were among the marching columns.

Home in Paris once more after the long Prussian and Polish campaigns (he loved the long campaigns), Bonaparte was soon enough restless and unsettled in his domestic day-to-day and the banal affairs of state. Divorcing Josephine was on his mind too, of course, and his libido (given greater concessions) was as keen as ever to roam. Naturally, like his maréchals and générals and hundreds of weary campaign officers, he succumbed easily and willingly to the gossipy, scented, velvet world of Parisian boudoirs. And just as naturally, and like all despotically inclined rulers, he indulged fantastic ideas as they occurred to him (with no regard to repercussions) and set about bedding the willing young ladies who presented themselves, nowadays, with little ceremony or subtlety. To conquer! To enact the will! For this was the way Bonaparte saw each successive moment that made up his life: an accumulation of moments and each an opportunity for victory, loss or surrender. 'It is a simple thing,' he often said to Talleyrand, 'to act! You *philosophes* have never understood!'

As soon as Général Junot was gone, the Emperor had in mind to seduce the man's wife again. An earlier encounter had been somewhat embarrassing (he'd drunk too much champagne) and he was determined to redeem himself.

In a stroke of luck for Junot's beautiful wife, who doubted she had the strength to resist Bonaparte, or, failing that, to pretend that he was irresistible (rejecting the little man was fraught with all sorts of unpleasantness), a ball held at Fontainebleau provided a formidable distraction in the fresh, bosomy form of Dominique-Adèle de Papillard, Comtesse d'Anjou, a pretty young thing who loved to flirt and be seduced in turn. Sparks flew when the Emperor noticed the comtesse and soon enough he was there beside her, gracing her with his full attention. A relieved Madame Junot (her husband would have called the comtesse a successful military diversion) was able to enjoy the ball and eventually leave with her own lover, the much younger, more brilliantly capable and far better endowed Major Louis-Armand Chaptelle.

Talleyrand saw what was happening (in fact had always known that it would happen) and leaned over to whisper in Bonaparte's ear.

'I have been told she has an itch, sire,' he said in a low voice, smiling across at the breezy, laughing Comtesse d'Anjou, who sat on the other side of Bonaparte now, her hand already resting on his arm. 'An itch where she should not.'

Bonaparte turned to his bishop.

'In this instance, sire, it might be best to consider a tactical retreat.' *And not act the fool.*

'Very good, Talleyrand,' Bonaparte said. He nodded solemnly, disappointed, and left the ball soon after.

The following day, he bestowed upon his bishop the new title of His Serene Highness, Prince de Bénévent and Vice-Grand Elector et cetera, et cetera. Seemed the *philosophes* knew a thing or two as well.

And on the long march to the peninsula with Général Jean-Andoche Junot, strange coincidences and converging events, though there were no Talleyrands to warn the unsuspecting, horny soul how to act.

'I've got the itch!' Wolfie said, putting a hand down the front of his pants and scratching vigorously. The men laughed, and so did Johannes.

'The girl in Angoulême?' someone said.

'By Christ!'

Johannes began on the drum and the men fell into song.

'The girl from Angoulême, by Christ! The girl from Angoulême!'

THE COLEOPTERIST

The 4e Régiment Étrangers were marched south-west, back across Poland and Prussia and all the way down through France (including Angoulême), about thirteen hundred miles or thereabouts to the Pyrénées, then up and over the mountains into Spain, and then further on, finally, into Portugal.

Along the way, men bandaged their feet and treated their sores, cut and bled their swollen blisters and shoved army communiqués into their boots for padding. They stole food and liquor and seduced village daughters (there were rapists, too), helped themselves to horses and sheep and wheels of cheese. Other men deserted and disappeared, as though blown off the marching columns by a sudden gust of wind, as easily as dust.

Johannes Meyer ran twice (against Wolfie's advice) and was caught twice and both times he was beaten with a cane. He was fortunate to live (it was considered bad luck to execute a drummer) but he hardly seemed to appreciate his position.

Every other deserter who'd been caught was shot by firing squad, their trials over within seconds; just a reading-out of the inexcusable crime and then the musket salvo and their bodies dragged away into a greasy ditch.

Wolfie grew exasperated. 'You'll take it too far,' he said. 'The drums won't save you forever.' He didn't think the boy had it in him to survive on his own, a fugitive.

'Next time I won't get caught.'

'Where do you think you're going anyway?' Wolfie said. 'What, there's a young princess waiting for you somewhere, in an enchanted castle? She makes the best dumplings in the world and all she wants to do is feed and fuck you?'

'Come with me,' Johannes said. 'She's got a sister.'

'They'll shoot you eventually! Don't you understand?'

But Johannes Meyer simply didn't care anymore.

Wolfie had many contacts in the Grande Armée, similarly keen and cunning men, of sharp eye and moral indifference. Through these subterranean associations he'd been able to procure tobacco, brandy, meat, new boots—even a lotion for his itch. He'd also come to hear about Colonel Pierre François Marie Auguste Dejean, a count and a uniquely mild man, loved by his soldiers and, as it turned out, a committed collector of beetles, willing to pay cash for any six-legged specimens that came a soldier's way. To distract Johannes from trying to run off and get himself shot, Wolfie convinced him to catch beetles for the colonel.

'You'll get pins, glass vials and boxes,' Wolfie said. His heart gladdened when he saw interest spark in the boy's eyes (it was a memory, the room in Berlin filled with specimens and cabinets, and Beatrice, and the girl, yes, the other girl in the window).

'Scientific equipment?' Johannes said. 'Out here?'

'I just said, didn't I?'

Johannes looked into Wolfie's eyes, which were the colour of rain clouds. And then his friend smiled and his face broke into a thousand granite lines and crevices and crags. And there in all that stone, in all those sharp planes and weathered edges, Johannes saw the kindest face that had ever been shown him before.

'Trust me,' Wolfie said. He patted Johannes on the shoulder, then pushed him away, unable to endure his own affection for the boy.

A few days later, a lieutenant from Colonel Dejean's regiment came with the equipment. His name was Gustave and he showed Johannes how to glue pieces of cork into the inside top of his shako and then pin the beetles there as he found them.

'Just try not to get shot or blown up,' Gustave said. 'At least, not until you've got the specimens to us.' His face was serious. 'And understand the difference in species. We don't need any *Porcellio scaber*, or that kind of thing, right? Don't bring me any of that crustacean in the order of Isopoda shit, because I'm not interested. What we want is beetles, in the order of Coleoptera, so count the fucking legs, for Christ's sake, right? Anything over six, forget about it.'

Johannes Meyer began collecting beetles.

The days were no longer an eternity. They possessed a beginning, a middle and an end. The nights, too, passed restful and dreamless. Hunting for the beetles took his mind off war and death. The world acquired scale again.

And he fell in love with the beetles. They were little gods in gleaming armour, blue-black and purple, red and coppery bronze, iridescent, beautiful. Johannes was disappointed at having to hand them over ('It's money!' Wolfie said) and so he began to sketch them in a notebook that Wolfie procured for him, along with a nib and a bottle of India ink.

Johannes Meyer proved skilful in catching them. During the action at Óbidos he caught seven different varieties. The following day, at Roliça, he found five more while marching through the dry, flinty gullies in the hills overlooking the village. He pinned them all inside his shako and looked forward to drawing them in his notebook that night. But then the battle began mid-morning and went on for hours and he had to forgo that happiness until the fighting was over.

The Battle of Roliça was a slaughter and the outnumbered French were defeated. They suffered seven hundred casualties, the English and Portuguese four hundred and eighty-five. The last Johannes had seen of Wolfie was during the assault by the 29th Regiment of Foot (the brazen English charge up the hill), an attack the French had initially repulsed and almost turned to victory, but there was a second full-frontal assault immediately after the first and then it was all over. Johannes had drummed the men down into the fray and he'd seen Wolfie charge at the English with his bayoneted musket, but then he'd lost him in the cannon smoke.

In the morning, the Portuguese peasants came with their donkeys and rough boarded carts, dead soldiers stacked in the trays. It took a number of trips to collect and deliver them all, it was miserable work, but the villagers of Roliça didn't want the bodies strewn over their hills and in the gullies, and nor did they think it was their duty to bury so many dead into the dry, hard-packed earth. They delivered them and said, 'Here are your soldiers,' and waited for coins, standing beside the carts. They were poor and some of them had looted the bodies, but not all, and they hoped for payment because bringing the bodies up was respectful and dignified them.

Général Delaborde sent a man around with a shako and the small collection was handed to the peasants. They took their empty carts back down to the village.

The sun was already blazing and there were many flies. The soldiers drew lots for who'd wield the shovels and picks first, then tied handkerchiefs over their noses and mouths like bandits. Johannes found Wolfie in one of the lines of bodies on the ground. Wolfie's arm had been blown off at the elbow and his belly was bloody, chewed up with shrapnel.

Later that night, under a cold scattered belt of stars, Johannes took his notebook and his collection of beetles, some water, a bayonet and a loaf of bread, and took off into the silvered darkness, and nobody caught him this time as he set off alone through the pine stands in the hills behind the camp. He'd never play a drum again.

TO KILL A MAN IS NOTHING

Through pure luck and the adrenaline of fear, they managed to eventually drag themselves to the small town of Borken. Exhausted.

They'd strapped Mr Hendrik's leg and made a crutch, then stumbled on for miles, across fields and through groves of birch, oak and pine, along muddy trails pressed with small animal prints in stuttering diagonal lines, down empty, stonewalled lanes in the middle of the night. Mostly, Krüger carried Mr Hendrik on his back (he was feverish and unable to walk without intense pain). It was all impossible and pointless, and often when they stopped to rest the burden of their bodies almost crushed their will. And yet neither man complained. They went on. They endured together. They exchanged barely a word (what was there to say?), but the silence between them deepened and fused their plight. The silence contained the truth of their presence inside it, nobody else in the whole wide world but them. They, exclusively, shared what they had created, and had created what they shared. It was not the intimacy of brothers (nor of lovers) but of friends, willingly beholden.

They slept in abandoned houses without roofs, with sheep and cows in cold barns, out in the open sometimes, even on the harshest nights. They had initially avoided villages and towns and had drawn out the distance between themselves and the carriage (and the body of Wesley Lewis Jr) for as long as they were able. One night, finally, an inn on the outskirts of Borken: a meal and a bed, safe enough now, surely. It was the first bed they'd slept in for weeks. A cold night, but their blankets were warm, even if they were wretched and Mr Hendrik's leg had turned a shade of deep purple.

They ate and went to sleep. And then, in the moon dark, a man.

Krüger woke with a lamp in his face and the barrel of a pistol pressed into his cheek.

'*Shhh . . .*' a voice said. 'Not a word now, son.'

Instinctively, no idea where he was, Krüger tried to lift his head. The pistol pressed him harder. The flintlock creaked, steel and spring stretching, Krüger felt the tensing through his skull; then a *click*, the pistol primed, alive. He was unable to formulate one succinct thought.

'Nice and calm,' the voice said. 'There's a man at the door, too.'

In the next bunk, Mr Hendrik said, 'Not him.'

The room had gathered a soft, honeyed light from around the cruel lamp. Krüger's eyes adjusted. He saw an older man with long grey hair and white stubble thick over his chin, face deeply grained. He wore a dark coat with gold military buttons, the shoulders with faded rectangles where epaulettes had once been sewn. His shadow stretched the full length of the room and loomed above them.

'You killed the American?' he said, the pistol still at Krüger's temple, though he was looking over at Mr Hendrik now.

'To kill a man is nothing.'

The tall dark shadow smiled. 'Well, black man, you'll be finding out soon enough.'

THE WORLD IS ALWAYS
DIFFERENT IN THE DARK

Elisabeth von Hoffmann opened her eyes and, for a brief disconcerting moment, had to remember where she was (a hotel, Bordeaux). She slipped out of bed without waking the général. She'd had a dream.

Elisabeth lit a candle and sat down at the dresser. In the mirror, she gazed at her face. The dream had returned her to a window in Berlin, the day Napoleon Bonaparte marched through the Brandenburg Gate, the day she'd seen the boy, the one who'd looked up at her from the couch. This time, in the dream, he didn't look up and Elisabeth had waited at the window, desperate for his eyes, for his head to turn in her direction. Somebody was tugging at her arm at the same time (it was the man she'd seen, with the arms pinned like a bird, she remembered). He was trying to pull her away, yet Elisabeth knew that she had to see the boy look up, it was an explicit requirement of the dream, and she couldn't go before he had. Even inside the dream, she knew that it had happened before in real life, but it was crucial that it happen again.

She held her ground, resisted, but the boy didn't turn around. She waited a few moments more, then relinquished to the pull at her arm. She allowed the man to drag her away. That was when she woke up.

The candle flame on the dresser flickered in the corner of Elisabeth's eye. She glanced at it, the space of a breath, then looked back into the mirror. Now, suddenly, it was the boy she saw reflected back at her. She blinked and he was gone.

In the morning, Bordeaux was rainy. By late afternoon, the ships in the port were bare-masted and ghost-like in the grey mist. Elisabeth, Général Fourés and his aide-de-camp,

Christophe Bergerard (whom the général had been able to retain), were drinking *vin chaud* in the hotel, waiting to board.

'It will do you good,' the général said to Elisabeth.

'Yes.'

'I only hope the journey won't make you worse.'

'It's nothing,' Elisabeth said. 'A cold. I'll be fine.'

'You said that earlier and now you look worse. Doesn't she, Bergerard?'

'Maybe the same, Mademoiselle?'

'Better!' Elisabeth smiled. She picked up her *vin chaud*. 'To your health, gentlemen.'

'To yours,' Fourés said seriously. 'I want the colour back in those cheeks!'

Bergerard finished his wine and stood. 'I'd better see to our luggage, Général. It's nearly time.'

'Good, Christophe. And tell Captain Mènard I wish to speak to him onboard.'

'Yes, Général.'

Fourés had been informed of British naval movements in the wider Caribbean and of attacks on French ports and trading vessels. They were to be accompanied by two forty-gun frigates, but the warships would eventually turn towards Martinique, leaving them alone for the last leg of the journey. Général Fourés thought about these things, and distracted himself with them, but really he was nervous because he'd never sailed before in his life. Forty days at sea! Under his cloak, he was sweating. Last night he'd dreamed of sinking ships. He wished for his horse.

'I hope the weather improves,' Elisabeth said.

Fourés nodded. They sipped their hot wine and waited for Bergerard to return.

GRILLED SARDINES

On a beach in San Sebastián, Johannes Meyer sat and watched the sea for a whole afternoon, boots off and trousers rolled above his ankles, raw toes numb in the cold sand.

The rushing sound of the waves, his eyes trying to follow, put him in a trance, but he was unable to forget completely about the wicker baskets he'd seen at the docks, filled with anchovies and sardines like briny jewels, and the barefoot fishermen, brown as leather, eyes small and liquid, passing the baskets up from the boats, the fish sliding and glistening, white-bellied and silver and black, streaks of red blood bright at their gills. And the man grilling sardines by the sea wall, the smell of the fragrant, unbearable, oily charred smoke.

Johannes Meyer fell asleep and woke a couple of hours later, his hunger intact and even more intense.

The sky glowed at the fold of evening and night. The moon was a perfect, clean white curve. The waves curled and crashed. He thought of the man called Krüger, who'd said that all destinations were inevitable. That the whole earth was a single entity, that each one of us was a mere hair strand of its memory. Johannes had never been to the sea before, but it seemed there was something here that he remembered.

The second time he went to where the fishermen were, he bartered his bayonet for the grilled sardines. When Johannes tasted the crisp charred skin, the flaking, clean salty flesh and the oil moistening the inside of his mouth, his cracked lips, he realised it was this that he remembered, though he'd never eaten grilled sardines before in his life.

He asked the man if there were any boats he could earn passage on.

'To where?'

'Anywhere,' Johannes said.

The man smiled. 'Only fishing boats, friend. They do not go far.'

Seeing how the boy had relished the fish, he gave Johannes a few more sardines.

'For the knife,' he said. 'I see now that it is a very good knife.'

The man went about his work, gutting the soft white bellies and pulling gills, scraping scales. He whistled as he cleaned the fish, called out to people and sold the grilled sardines to them, drank from a wineskin, squirting the liquid into his open mouth. Johannes finished eating and sat for a while in the sun and watched the boats and the fishermen on the docks.

When the man packed up his grill and kicked sand over the coals, he slapped Johannes on the shoulder. 'May the Virgin protect you, friend.'

The high treacherous roads at the border were busy with French troops marching into Spain, but Johannes managed to get through. He made it to the outskirts of Bordeaux. He'd hoped to find a ship there, but barely escaped being arrested in La Brède (gangs were rounding up peasants to replenish the ranks of the Grande Armée) and he had to give the idea up. His luck held for another three hundred miles, but in a little town not far from Paris, the war caught up with him again.

After his arrest, it was discovered that Johannes was a deserter. Records were summoned and decisions made. A lieutenant by the name of Duval confiscated his collection of beetles and took the notebook with all his drawings. He gave Johannes a uniform and said, 'A fair exchange, no?' He didn't smile. Then he sent Johannes Meyer to Holland, to fight against the English once more.

THE STORM

Elisabeth von Hoffmann stood on the deck of the *Anne-Laure* and looked out over the sparkling sea, calm now after the storm. The sky was an enormous blue dome, the horizon glaring white in every direction. She stood with confidence, tall, proud and not a little euphoric.

Général Fourés was still in their cabin, suffering. Last night's storm had emptied both his stomach and spirit. It had done so for many on the ship, even a few of the old sailors who'd seen every kind of sea, but Elisabeth had endured and of all the passengers on board today she appeared fresh and even rejuvenated on deck. The sailors acknowledged her, no words, just small smiles and winks.

Sure-footed, planted, the deepest surges of the ship, the deepest currents of the sea, it had all come up through Elisabeth's feet and she'd felt as firm as a rod of iron. And supple too, intuitive. If it weren't for dresses and propriety and women's shoes, she'd have climbed the rigging barefoot, right to the top of the mast.

The wind, the waves muscling the ship; last night it had lifted like a wing on the swelling sea, breached the foam ridges of surging heights, and then plunged down the steep trough slopes, crashing into the dark sea valleys, over and over. Down, then up, up again, men scrambling over the deck, pulling ropes, calling out and holding on, the rigging whipped and howling, the long groans of the hull timbers. But Elisabeth had never doubted, not the ship, not her survival. She had no explanation for her certainty.

And now the storm seemed to her a culmination, the end of an old life and the beginning of something new. She was at the mercy of wind and water and there were no fixed points. And she wasn't frightened, because she was free.

THE DEBT AND THE PRICE

Some time later, when things had settled, Krüger took a position teaching German at the local school in Borken. The council itself had approached him and made the offer.

The five children who came to his class (aged between six and ten) were unenthusiastic. They weren't interested in learning to write and speak grammatically. Their parents were mostly poor farmers and made them work before and after school. None of them would be there long enough to learn much, and nobody they knew spoke that way besides.

Krüger discovered that what they liked best was having stories read to them and soon that became the whole lesson, which made things easier for everyone. His heart wasn't in the teaching, it was an agony, but reading the stories had turned into an unexpected pleasure. The narratives surprised him with their artistry and craft, and then there was also the particular feeling of joy when he saw the children so enraptured, hanging on every word he read, their faces raw with tension, every heart hooked in a bundle of lines running to the book in Krüger's hands.

He still had a room at the same inn where the bounty hunter had come that night and arrested Mr Hendrik (how the man had discovered them, Krüger still had no clue). He spent his evenings choosing stories to read for the children. He waited for Mr Hendrik's trial. He ate only a little bread and cheese, sometimes an apple, drank white wine, which he indulged in (it was crisp and sweet and pale yellow like straw) for only then could he sleep. He tried to write, but each word was like a hair plucked out of his arm.

The whole town knew what had happened, of course, but it was impossible for these upstanding folk to imagine a Prussian involved in gruesome murder, such as the case was. Krüger was seen as an unfortunate and innocent bystander to the whole business.

'The Negro and the American were a party,' the carriage driver said when the trial finally began. 'They'd paid for the journey together.'

'How would you describe their relations?'

'They were plainly in a state of some animosity towards one another.'

'And Herr Krüger?' the magistrate said.

'Herr Krüger joined the coach separately. He kept to himself and read his books.'

Nobody questioned why Krüger had helped the lame Negro get all the way to Borken ('Because he's a good Christian!' they said). The verdict was speedy and unanimous. The murderous, crippled Negro was sentenced to death by hanging.

Weeks passed and then months, and they were still waiting for the executioner to arrive from Recklinghausen. And then that moment inevitably arrived, too.

Krüger went to see Mr Hendrik. He had no idea what to bring. He brought an apple and a piece of cheese and a bottle of white wine.

The gaoler led him along a short corridor of cells and then unlocked a heavy timber door. Inside, Mr Hendrik was lying on empty grain sacks on the flagstone floor. As he dragged himself up, the gaoler locked them both in together.

The cell was cold. Mortar crumbled out of the damp walls. Mr Hendrik was thin and sallow and there was a patchy beard over his chin. They'd taken his clothes, shoes, given him a coarse grey woollen tunic and pants, all of it filthy. There was a slop bucket in the corner, straw over the floor. His lame and broken leg was swollen around the knee and he held it straight out before him, gently rubbing his thigh.

'Tomorrow then,' Mr Hendrik said.

Krüger hesitated. 'Yes.'

Mr Hendrik stopped rubbing his leg, stared down at it. 'So,' he said. Then to himself, in Surinamese, *I have run further than any of them.*

Krüger reached into his pockets, took out the apple and the piece of cheese and put them down next to Mr Hendrik.

'Do you still have the Bible?'

'Yes,' Krüger said. 'I've spent nothing of it.' He wanted Mr Hendrik to know.

'You will buy Josephine with the gold.'

Krüger said nothing, only looked at Mr Hendrik blankly.

'She will not run with you,' Mr Hendrik said, 'you cannot save her. You must buy her from Captain van der Velde. To free her you must own her. It is the only way she will understand it.'

'Your sister is on the other side of the world.'

'And she is waiting for me. Now you.'

Somebody walked past the door. They listened to the footsteps fade.

'I've been wanting to bribe the gaolers,' Krüger said quietly, 'to get you out, but I wasn't—'

'No!' Mr Hendrik said, frowning, pointing at Krüger. 'You would lose the money and achieve nothing.'

Krüger nodded. 'Yes,' he said. In the cell, standing before Mr Hendrik, he felt it for the first time now, truly, that there was some purpose to his life. How could it possibly be this? But there it was.

He said, 'How will I find her?'

'There is a man in Paramaribo who will help you. His name is Bayman Quince Rotterdam. Can you remember?'

'Yes.'

'Everybody knows who he is. You can ask at any tavern. He is a sly, corrupt old black devil and he'll want to be paid and fed, but he will lead you to Josephine.'

Krüger took the bottle from his coat pocket and sat down next to Mr Hendrik. He leaned back against the cell wall and handed the doomed man the wine. After Mr Hendrik had drunk from it, he put the bottle to his own lips, but the wine was tasteless.

'You must do this for me,' Mr Hendrik said.

'I will do it.'

'Your word? This is what your people give?'

'You have it.'

Mr Hendrik reached behind his head, took the *obia* from around his neck and gave it to Krüger.

'Remember to believe,' he said.

Mr Hendrik was hanged the next morning. Krüger did not attend because he had already gone. Apart from the gaolers and the executioner from Recklinghausen, there was nobody else to come.

Mr Hendrik was buried in an unmarked grave in a field beyond the cemetery reserved for suicides and the variously mad and possessed.

It rained in Borken for the rest of the week.

BOOK V

THE SHRUNKEN HEAD

Claus von Rolt was asked (by a syrupy-eyed old general in exile) to accompany the Prussian envoy Ludwig von Kleist to London on a secret mission to secure armaments and raise funds for a planned rebellion against the French. Rolt was known to have spent time in the English capital and, along with his contacts, exemplary English and reputation for charm and wit, it was hoped his presence would soften the brusque military manner of von Kleist. Rolt accepted, of course, for there was no real choice; there was the appearance of patriotic duty to consider. There was also the opportunity to extricate himself from an *affaire d'amour* run its course. And there was the possibility of conducting a little business in rare species, London being the epicentre of the trade.

He packed his trunk and arrived on a clear, crisp Tuesday. It was 4 April 1809.

Rolt spent most of his days in meetings and dinners with one cabinet minister after another, listening to von Kleist as he tried to sell the Prussian plan and receive a pledge from the English. After three weeks, they were no closer to any kind of commitment, and then they heard the Austrians were in town too, seeking assistance for their own uprising (bigger and better than the comparatively vague Prussian plan). After that, Ludwig von Kleist became quite desperate and pushy. Rolt knew this wasn't the approach to take with the English. They nodded politely into their soup as von Kleist argued his case. They cleared their throats as the plates were taken from between Kleist's firmly planted elbows, and they smiled uncomfortably and tried to change the subject, and still he insisted. Finally, they listened to von Kleist beg and were forced to say, 'We'll see what we can do,' and hoped the man would desist from embarrassing himself and those around him any further.

The shrunken head was in a glass cabinet at Lord Oldham's house.

They were in his study, drinking French cognac after dinner, and like all the dukes and lords before him, Lord Oldham had stopped listening to what von Kleist had to say. The shrunken head hung by a braided cord from a small brass hook, like the pendulum in some grotesque clock, a blackened leathery ball about the size of a fist. It had long matted hair and wide, shrivelled lips sewn unevenly together, as were the half-closed eyelids, bulging and puckered around the thread, and the nose upturned like a snout, the nostrils obscenely flared. Its cheeks were sunken and lacerated and the face was dry and tight, knuckled like a ham hock. Claus von Rolt couldn't take his eyes off it.

'My son brought it back for me,' Lord Oldham said, noticing the Prussian's interest and keen for the distraction from the insufferable von Kleist. 'South America, I believe. They're into that sort of thing down there you know—lopping off the enemy's head and usurping its power. If only it were that easy!'

'Savages,' Ludwig von Kleist said. 'Cannibals.'

'I've often wondered what his name was,' Lord Oldham said. 'My wife calls him Richard.'

'How is it done?' Rolt said.

'First the skull is removed and the flesh cut away, then they fill it with heated pebbles and sand and sew everything back up again. Leave the head to dry and wait until the whole thing shrinks. Hell of a job. Then they wear the heads around their necks and apparently become invincible—or invisible. One or the other. Useless either way, I should think.'

'What would you take, Lord Oldham,' Rolt said, 'if I were to make an offer?'

'For my old friend Richard?'

'Name a price, sir. I will endeavour to oblige.'

'Ha! And I thought you Prussians had no money!'

WAR CONTINUES IN THE CARIBBEAN, TOO

The *Anne-Laure* was taken without a single cannon being fired, slightly north-west and ten nautical miles from Cayenne.

'What would be the point of engagement?' Captain Mènard had said, looking out at the three enemy ships sailing towards him. 'There's nowhere to escape, except to the bottom.'

'Make a run for it, sir?' his first officer said. 'Back out to sea?'

'Your enthusiasm isn't matched by our abilities, Augustin. And we've only a day's fresh water left, maybe two.'

Général Fourés agreed. 'It would be a pointless risk.' The frigates had long since left them and, besides, the British and Portuguese had already occupied the colony. The général shook his head, patted the captain on the back. 'You got us here safely,' he said. 'Best we continue the course.'

'Augustin,' Captain Mènard said to the first officer, 'strike the colours.'

The enemy ships held back and then a launch was sent over from the brig *Vingança*. Half-a-dozen Portuguese soldiers boarded the *Anne-Laure*. Their lieutenant was a short but erect man with a thin moustache, in riding boots and spurs. He approached Captain Mènard and saluted. In a loud, theatrical voice, he asked the captain to surrender his ship. Mènard did so, squaring up his shoulders, and then along with Général Fourés he led the Portuguese lieutenant into his cabin.

'What happens now?' Elisabeth von Hoffmann asked. It was very bright on deck and hot, and she shaded her eyes with her hand.

Christophe Bergerard said, 'They take the ship and put a Portuguese flag on her.'

'I mean to us.'

Bergerard shrugged.

When the three men emerged from the captain's cabin a short while later, the Portuguese lieutenant called over two of his soldiers. They stood to attention on either side of Général Fourés. The général removed his sword and presented it in both hands to the Portuguese lieutenant, who bowed formally and took it. The général was then politely arrested as a prisoner of war and escorted across the deck by the soldiers.

Elisabeth hurried over to him.

'Michel—'

'It's all right, *ma chérie*,' the général said, trying to appear relaxed. 'Just games we are obliged to play.'

He took her hand. Fourés was still pale, clammy and exhausted (it had been, in the end, fifty-nine days at sea), and he'd lost weight during the trip. He suddenly seemed much older to Elisabeth, frail and feeble in his loose-fitting uniform.

'What should I do?' she said.

'Rest, be calm and wait for me. Captain Mènard will get you ashore and Christophe can take care of everything until I return.'

Elisabeth hugged the général tightly and whispered in his ear, *'I love you.'*

'Wait for me,' he said. 'Yes?'

She stepped back and watched him walk over to the side of the ship. The général paused and nodded to her, then disappeared down the rope ladder.

LIKE A GRIEVING MAN

On the horizon, a black speck sailed across the white line of sky and sea, bound the long way for Paramaribo after erratic winds and waters had forced a change of course. From its decks and with the naked eye, it was impossible to see the *Anne-Laure* (its opposite and equal black speck) clearly, to see it being boarded by the Portuguese and the général arrested and descending the rope ladder, or Elisabeth von Hoffmann on deck, uncertain and yet enthralled by the circumstances in motion that were her life now. Impossible to see and yet Krüger was looking exactly in that direction as Elisabeth stood and experienced her presence in the world as though for the first time. He was gazing intently down the invisible line that linked their momentary cartographic perfections of latitude and longitude, two lives only a few nautical miles apart and yet unknown to each other (though of course the gods knew them both).

Krüger, as he stood there on the deck contemplating the sea, sank into the feeling of his unboundedness, blissfully adrift. The ship had taken his life out of his hands and placed it at the whim of air and water. He was free and the sensation overwhelmed his inner self. Air and water, endless, simple, content, all that it took to be free! But Krüger didn't consider that these were gods too, old gods waiting around, frolicking, playing, shouldering and enforcing, nature at their fingertips, nature soothed, pressed, palpitated, struck (raging Tiamat of the saltwater seas and thunderous Tlaloc of the rain, Enlil the sky god, wielder of storms, the sisters called Djunkgao who stroked the ocean currents with the palms of their hands). Krüger sensed these otherworldly forces (who cannot sense them?) but could not forge the words that might describe them. Without words, he was denied their dimensions, and thus their maps could not be drawn by his imagination and they eluded him. And so Krüger remained upon the surface of things. Like a grieving man, he understood his relief as freedom from the world that had grieved him, rather than a deeper immersion, as young Elisabeth von Hoffmann had understood it, as she had understood it during her own relief, in the aftermath of her own storm of gods. She was inside and present and Krüger was on the surface of things and absent, yet to understand the true dimensions of the world.

'What are you looking at?' Christophe Bergerard said.

Elisabeth shrugged, squinting across the bright blue ocean, a hand over her eyes against the glare, towards a small dark smudge on the horizon. She'd turned just then and looked out and there it was, as though it had called to her. 'Is that a ship?' she said.

THE GUILLOTINE

The *Anne-Laure* was brought in under escort and dropped anchor about a mile out from the settlement. Everybody then waited onboard for what seemed an excessively long time before they were allowed to disembark. Even the Portuguese lieutenant began to pace the deck and grumble at his men.

'Signal them again!' he said.

'Yes, sir!'

Bureaucratic matters were eventually resolved and a launch sailed Elisabeth and Christophe into the Cayenne docks. (Captain Mènard had kissed her vigorously. 'My best sailor! Goodbye!') The water was choppy and splashed over the bow, drenching Elisabeth's dress down her left side. Ahead of them, Cayenne was cut into dense green forest that stretched out endlessly around it. Already, its humid, heavy presence could be felt, even inside the cool threading of sea breezes.

A man by the name of Dr Antoine Girodet was waiting for them. He introduced himself and apologised for the lacklustre welcome.

'We have been defeated and occupied,' he said, 'and our administration has succumbed to its habitual indifference, only more so. It's the weather, you see.' He turned to Elisabeth. 'I'm sorry for the loss of your général, Mademoiselle.'

'Do you know where they've taken him?'

'Where? No.'

Elisabeth narrowed her eyes at Girodet. He was olive-skinned, with dark unruly hair, young and handsome (she admitted it, though there was something about him that she immediately didn't like). 'No,' she said, echoing him softly.

'Wait!' Girodet suddenly said, calling out over her shoulder and making Elisabeth jump. 'Is that the blade?'

Behind Elisabeth, sailors were unloading crates from another launch that had come from the *Anne-Laure*. Girodet walked quickly towards them. He spoke with the sailors and then pointed to a nearby cart. Elisabeth saw two Indians (she thought they must be) standing in front of it, shoulders harnessed like horses and naked except for barely covered loins. Their flat, red-brown faces were blank, inscrutable. She thought they looked like children.

Girodet directed the sailors among the items unloaded from the launch. They eventually carried over a large flat crate and two smaller ones, as well as a few long lengths of dark timber. They stacked everything into the cart and then the doctor slipped them a bottle of rum.

'Who is this Dr Girodet?' Elisabeth said.

Christophe had sat down on one of their trunks (the heat was unbelievable) and removed his coat. 'We'll find out, I suppose.'

Dr Girodet came back to them, his sweaty face bright with excitement. 'We can walk,' he said. 'It's not far. You can put your luggage in the cart.'

'Walk where?' Elisabeth said.

'To my humble home, Mademoiselle, of course. I shall have the honour of your presence until matters with the Portuguese, and your accommodation, become a little clearer.'

Their luggage was loaded into the cart and the two Indians began to pull and the three of them followed behind as it moved off, wheels grinding and wobbly. Girodet offered Elisabeth an umbrella for shade, but she declined.

'Do you know,' the doctor said, opening the umbrella above his own head, 'the blade in that large crate right there took the heads of King Louis and Queen Marie Antoinette?'

Bergerard looked over at Girodet.

'The very blade,' the doctor said. 'Incredible, no?'

'My father was there,' Bergerard said. 'At the place de la Révolution.'

'Truly?' Girodet smiled, showing small bright teeth. 'But that is wonderful!'

FLUSHING FEVER

On the evening of 14 August 1809, the British navy (commanded by Sir Richard Strachan, 6th Baronet) resumed an intense bombardment of the Dutch port town of Flushing, where a significant portion of Bonaparte's navy was stationed. That same night, under the smoke and flash and boom of their guns, with the town in flames and the French retreating and much confusion in the streets, Johannes Meyer slipped away from his regiment.

He reached the banks of the River Scheldt just before dawn and found a small raft normally used for poling cargo to and from the riverboats. He dragged it into the water and then, staying as low as possible on his knees, he poled the raft across the river to the island of Walcheren. The British were stationed there, with an army of forty thousand men.

As he neared the island, Johannes slipped into the water and waded through the freezing river to the shore. He walked a short distance, and when he saw the British soldiers he put his arms in the air and called out to them.

'I'm Prussian!'

The soldiers fired at him (twice; the shots thumped into the sand to his left and right) and then they rushed Johannes and held him at bayonet point. They searched him roughly, pushed him around a little, gave a jab to his kidneys and then walked him up to the main encampment. He was placed under guard in a small wooden shelter.

Men, cannon, equipment, wagons, horses, everywhere Johannes looked. There were ships anchored out in the deeper part of the estuary, sails tucked away, and further behind there was Flushing, on fire, pouring thick smoke into the air.

Johannes emptied his boots of water. He waited. Soon he noticed there were lots of men being carried around on stretchers, arms hanging limp off the sides. They moaned and looked feverish. Some of the men on the stretchers were silent and their faces were covered with tunics.

Half an hour later, an officer came to question Johannes. He wore a tasselled sword and knee-high boots and silver spurs, a tall Englishman in a well-tailored uniform, covered in far less mud than the soldiers Johannes had seen. He was clean-shaven but very pale and he sat down before Johannes with some weariness and a brief expression of pain. Then he asked questions in perfect German. Where was Johannes from and how had he come to be there? What was his regiment, who was his commanding officer? How many men did the French have, where else had he served? Was he a spy?

With the last question, the officer smiled.

'No,' Johannes said.

The Englishman nodded. 'From Berlin, you say?'

'Yes.'

'Tell me, is there still a tavern on Brüderstraße, towards the Schloßplatz end of the street, called the Win auf den?'

'I haven't been in Berlin for a long time,' Johannes said. 'But it was still there when the French arrested me.'

'Good,' the officer said. He stood up and patted Johannes on the shoulder. *'Das ist alles gut.'*

A little while later, a soldier came and handed Johannes a British uniform.

'Should fit,' he said and waited for Johannes to get dressed. The uniform proved short in the arms and legs. The soldier said, 'Oh well, mate.'

Johannes was led to another part of the camp and issued a rifle and ammunition, and then, with a signature and a salute, he was formally enlisted into the 2nd Light Battalion of the King's German Legion. Two days later, he was back in Flushing, part of the British infantry assault. The town was taken, but the effort proved a complete and colossal waste of time. The French fleet had already retreated to Antwerp even before the bombardment had begun.

Worse still, on the island of Walcheren, the British had been decimated by Flushing fever: a rampant, ruthless spread of malaria, typhoid and dysentery, which eventually killed four thousand men (barely one hundred were killed in action) and infected a further sixteen thousand. The campaign was reduced to a desperate evacuation of the dying.

Johannes Meyer remained miraculously uninfected. Some weeks later he was finally shipped across the Channel to the Sussex coast, to a town called Bexhill-on-Sea, where the King's German Legion had its training depot.

He began planning his escape the moment he arrived.

PARAMARIBO

The heat. And in the air, an intense fragrance of lemon and orange blossom.

The River Surinam was choked with ships, barges and launches, loading sugar, molasses, coffee, cacao, indigo and cotton all bound for Holland, and unloading flour, beef and pork, salted fish and spermaceti candles, timber, horses and slaves. Krüger walked and watched. His legs were shaky. It had been forty-seven days at sea and stepping onto land hadn't changed anything. The heat was inebriating.

A slave ship from the West African coast had unloaded some twenty-odd Negroes: men, boys, women, children, naked and shielding their eyes from the light. What was left of an original one hundred and forty souls. The breeze picked up the stink of their stale sweat, of their fear and hunger. In a huddle, they were ladled water from a bucket then handed bananas and oranges.

A voice called out, 'Wash 'em!'

While the Negroes continued to eat, buckets on ropes were dipped into the river and then hauled up and the water was splashed over them; five, ten, fifteen buckets of river water. The women rubbed their children's hair and cheeks, their necks and chests and backs. After they'd eaten the fruit and had been washed by the buckets of water, a man came with a smaller bucket and each Negro cupped out some of the coconut oil there and rubbed it into their skin. The women rubbed their children then themselves. Now the Negroes glistened and Krüger could see how the men were roped in muscles and the women were smooth-legged and shone and the children were long-limbed and shiny too.

He walked on.

There were some fine houses in Paramaribo, made of timber and brightly painted, two and sometimes three storeys. Along the streets there were orange, tamarind and lemon trees, bursting in bloom, and magnificent gilded carriages making their way, the drivers in full livery (in the heat!), the horses immaculately brushed, and there were finely dressed men and women strolling in embroidered silks and glossy velvets, gold and silver lace, the women with elegant French parasols to guard against the sun. Krüger had never seen anything like it.

At one corner a large group stood around a birdcage hung from a tree: inside, a black-and-red-feathered bird, barely the size of a thumb. It chirped and tweeted sharply. Krüger noticed wealthy gentlemen in expensive clothes, holding silver-tipped canes, and women in silks and lace, fanning themselves. There were barefoot slaves in worn breeches, too, and slave women smoking small wooden pipes. There were ragged children running about, black and white and every shade between, and men who stood importantly at the rear of the crowd, broad-rimmed hats low over their eyes, silent except for an occasional whisper into the ear of one of the slaves, who then ran over to a mulatto man standing beside the birdcage with a slate in his hands. Bets were made and a moment later the talking ceased and everybody fell silent and watched the birdcage.

A tall, skinny Negro came up close to the cage. The tiny bird inside flitted about. Once it had calmed and perched itself on a branch stuck between the cage bars, the Negro closed his eyes and licked his lips and began to whistle. It was a soft, low, beautiful sound. Krüger could see the Negro's thin, scarred cheeks quiver, just as though a bird's tiny heart was beating beneath its surface, and the sound he made trembled and carried on the heavy, humid air.

The bird in the cage looked about, its head moving in quick jerks. The people standing around waited and didn't move and watched the bird. It continued to perch there on the branch and jerk its little head and it didn't make a sound. And then, with a flurry of wings, it suddenly flew to the cage bars and gripped them and let out a harsh squawk.

The crowd exclaimed as one. Money quickly changed hands. Krüger asked and discovered: the object of the game was to inspire the bird to sing. It was called *rackling*.

'But this rackler no good!' the old slave beside him said.

Another man came up to the cage. Wagers were made.

Krüger moved on. At a nearby tavern he asked for Bayman Quince Rotterdam. He was told to wait, that Bayman would come by in the early afternoon.

ST GILES OF THE CRIPPLED AND INDIGENT

Claus von Rolt found the place off Brewer Street in Piccadilly. The proprietor's name was Hugh Alfred Collins. They'd met briefly many years before, over the sale of a Cuban crocodile (to an Italian prince), and then Rolt had dealt the man's work in Berlin a few more times (a squirrel monkey, a flamingo, a toucan, a leopard). Though they'd fetched good prices, Collins certainly wasn't the best taxidermist Rolt had ever seen. But his work managed to hold together, at least until the buyer had returned home with it, and he'd always been well connected with suppliers, from the legitimate naturalists and explorers with government funding (and a willingness to sell *spare* specimens to private collectors) to the wealthy eccentrics who insisted on hunting the rare species themselves, but tended to die during their naive and ill-equipped expeditions. Hugh Collins also had artistic aspirations; he wanted his work to capture life. Rolt was philosophically partial to the ambition.

He opened the front door. Inside, a barrage of smells: turpentine, arsenic, camphor, mould and dust; the animal smells of tanned skins and greasy fur; the musty, mangy smell of old feathers; the oiled linseed of wood and the smoked, tannin smell of leather. The place was in desperate need of an open window.

All around, on the floor and crowded onto tables and shelves, on top of narrow plinths, in the window ledges, there were animals in different poses: down on all fours or up on hind legs, calmly perched on branches or clawing at the bark with wings spread mid-flap, species both docile and baring their teeth. Some were only half complete and showed the wire construction in their chests and the hessian stuffing in their backs, their small, brown featherless wings and empty eye sockets waiting for coloured glass beads. It seemed business was solid for Hugh Alfred Collins.

Rolt walked through the silent animals. The dusty room felt poised, or frozen. He noted a number of rare species, including a *Platypus anatinus*, labelled with a tag on its webbed foot. He stopped before the strange creature, no more than a foot long.

'You're aware that Blumenbach named it *Ornithorhynchus paradoxus*, which is now the accepted designation?' Rolt asked. 'Has been for some time.'

'Of course a Prussian would say that,' Hugh Collins said, coming out from behind a worktable. There were red-and-yellow-feathered birds laid out there, surrounded by various hand tools, spools of thread and bowls of paste, brown bottles and vials of yellow-coloured liquid, a tin half filled with pellets. 'But I believe our Mr Shaw was first, Herr Rolt. One should always accept defeat graciously.'

Hugh Collins was lanky, broad-shouldered, a man of some thirty years. His sleeves were rolled up to the elbows, revealing large hands and hairy forearms wound in bulging veins, a man who might have swung a blacksmith's hammer rather than sit hunched over shot punctures in hummingbirds, delicately plugging them with cotton and resin. He wiped each of his fingers separately with a rag, then held out his hand.

Rolt shook his head. 'Let's not spread the arsenic around.'

'A little never hurt anybody.' Collins smiled and cracked his knuckles.

'Your work has become much finer, more expressive. Congratulations.'

'And priced accordingly, my friend.'

'How much for heads?' Rolt said.

Collins leaned back against the edge of the workbench. 'What sort?'

'Human. Shrunken.'

'Oh, righto then.' He crossed his arms. 'Well, there have been a few coming in from South America and the South Pacific lately. And from New Zealand now, too, or so they tell me.'

'You haven't come across any?'

Collins grimaced. 'One or two. Bloody awful things.'

Rolt extracted a small card from his pocket, the name of his hotel written there, and held it out to the taxidermist. 'You'll inform me?'

'Of course,' Collins said. 'But you know, they're already faking them. Dead whores from St Giles sold as South Pacific warriors named Akoni. Once they're dried and sewn up, they're all dark brown. Impossible to tell.'

'They're murdering people?'

Collins laughed. 'No need. The morgues are full of unclaimed bodies, there's plenty of stock. The Thames is practically choking on headless corpses.'

'I see.' Claus von Rolt combed the head of a tiny monkey with his forefinger. 'Then I must get to the original source.'

That week, Ludwig von Kleist finally heard back from the English. They'd committed the munitions requested, but had cut the fifty thousand pounds asked for down to twenty. Von Kleist was told, 'Be sure to use it wisely.' A letter of credit was written up.

'Finally,' von Kleist said, 'we can leave.'

'I think I'll stay a while longer, Herr Kleist,' Rolt said. 'I have some personal business to which I must attend.'

FOR THE GOOD OF MANKIND

Elisabeth von Hoffmann said, 'You want to know if the head of the decapitated man is capable of *seeing* anything?'

'Yes! And if they *feel*, if they sense anything else.' Dr Antoine Girodet paused, drank some wine, dabbed his lips with a napkin. 'Are they in pain? And, if so, where is the pain? What is the connection of the mind with the body? Where do feelings reside inside us? In the brain or the heart or in one's little toe?' Girodet smiled. 'Oh, there is much to be learned, Mademoiselle.'

'You hope the guillotined man's head will simply tell you all these things you wish to know, Dr Girodet?' Christophe Bergerard asked.

'Yes, Monsieur Bergerard—' Girodet looked over at the door and waved someone in '—that is it exactly.'

A dark mulatto girl came into the dining room and placed a silver platter of roasted meat on the table. Bergerard noticed how exceptionally beautiful the girl was and watched her walk away. Elisabeth had noticed her too.

'Roasted tapir,' Girodet said. 'You'll never eat pork again.'

They ate and drank and the wine was replenished and other dishes were brought in and placed on the table by the beautiful dark mulatto girl (sweet river fish, smoked eel, crabs). Insects smacked and winged the windows. The heat in the room was lifted and spread thinner by two rectangular, framed canvas sails hanging from the ceiling, operated by a bored Negro who stood near the door and pulled down on a rope, all the time staring at the floor.

'Who will be your participants?' Elisabeth von Hoffmann asked, disliking the stringy meat that had been served her as much as the topic of conversation.

'Slaves,' Girodet said. He waved his fork. 'Runaways.' He had an agent, apparently, in neighbouring Surinam, who procured Negro slaves on his behalf then smuggled them over the border, avoiding the Portuguese who were confiscating all healthy labour. It was how he'd acquired the young mulatto beauty serving the food this evening, though the agent had planned to keep her for himself. He'd asked a steep price, but Girodet had been unable to resist her.

'My work is for the human race,' he said. 'I am an explorer of the ultimate unknown frontier, on a perilous search for the bridge, for the window into the next world. Who can say what we might glimpse and discover?' Dr Antoine Girodet was sure it would make him famous.

Christophe nodded, intrigued. Elisabeth stared down at her plate.

'Have you heard of the eminent surgeon and philosopher Jacques de Dieu?' Girodet said to the young man. 'You must read his *Observations and Conclusions on the Post-decapitatory State of the Brain*. It was written in 1793, a magnificent enquiry into fibrillary contractions, corneal reflexes, the effects of severing the fourth cervical vertebrae and so on. He argued that it was indeed plausible there was a lingering of perception, of the eyes seeing and the brain comprehending, after the blade had done its work. And so, a moment of vision, quite possibly between life and death, no?'

'Or a moment of horror,' Elisabeth said.

Girodet smiled. 'We must find out! Can't you see?'

'And now you have your own blade.' She put down her knife and fork, pushed the plate away.

'I do indeed,' Girodet said. 'The blade of the Revolution!' He turned back to Christophe. 'Tell me, Monsieur Bergerard, are you squeamish about such things? I am in need of an assistant for my research.'

OH, HE'S DONE FOR NOW

Lieutenant Schneppen's main purpose in life was to action the use of his cane in the training and disciplining of his men—and right now, most particularly, his preoccupation was the exercising and disciplining of Johannes Meyer.

Schneppen had disliked the boy on sight (a deserter, a coward, tall) and the fact that he could barely hold a rifle correctly, took an eternity to reload and couldn't shoot a building if it was right there in front of him, drove Schneppen to near insanity. Johannes Meyer was a damning reflection on Prussia, whose defeat at the hands of the French still burned with bright shame in Lieutenant Schneppen's burly chest, a veteran of the lost Battle of Jena.

'A fucking *disgrace!*' he said.

The man's breath was hot with the pickled stench of an empty stomach. Johannes Meyer stood stock-still, sweating from the endless drills that morning, up and down the parade ground, up and down, up and down, his collarbone aching, and still it hadn't stopped. He was a thousand miles from everywhere. All the days since he'd arrived had been miserable, intolerable. The grey sky never clearing, the constant drizzle, the dull, penetrating cold that seemed to come up from deep in the ground. And Lieutenant Schneppen, his fellow Prussian, relentless and at his throat.

'Imbecile,' Schneppen said, this time in German. He struck Johannes with the cane. As the boy stumbled from the blow, Schneppen struck him again, right across his back.

The other soldiers stepped away. Johannes Meyer suddenly turned, stood and lunged for the lieutenant, crashed him to the ground. He scrambled over Schneppen in a fury, got his hands to the man's throat. Everything that had ever happened to him, every misfortune, here was the cause.

'He's going to kill him!'

'Do it!'

The two men struggled. Schneppen grimaced, made a tight, phlegmy, gargled sound. He took Johannes by the wrists but couldn't loosen the boy's hands on his throat.

The soldiers moved in around them.

Then, just as it appeared that Lieutenant Schneppen was about to take his last breath of damp English air, two ensigns pushed through the crowd of soldiers. The first one grabbed Johannes in a headlock, the other kicked him in the side. Still Johannes wouldn't let go. It took a second kick and a tightening of the headlock before he finally released the lieutenant.

More soldiers pushed through the men.

'Step aside!'

Lieutenant Schneppen was helped to his feet. He spat on the ground, coughed and spat again. He rubbed his neck and pointed at Johannes.

'Arrest him!' His voice was a thin, harsh whisper.

Johannes Meyer lunged, tried to attack the lieutenant again, but was held back. He was thumped in the stomach then dragged away to the guardhouse.

Somebody said, 'Oh, that's it. He's done for now.'

BAYMAN QUINCE ROTTERDAM

He said, 'Oh, Great Lord, by God, Good Lord Jesus Christ Our Saviour and King!' He took off his plumed, fur-trimmed cocked hat and held it to his chest. 'The lame one be dead! And the Devil take his soul and the Heaven be free of his wickedness!'

He was an old Negro with a huge barrel stomach and a black, silver-tipped cane, dressed in loose, torn stockings and worn heels and a long, dirty white wig that hung over his frayed admiral's epaulettes. The blue coat was trimmed in gold and silver, and the lace cuffs of his white shirt, gone yellow now from sweat and age, flowered at the wrists. Children had followed him into the tavern, street urchins laughing and running up to pull at his tails when he wasn't looking. Every now and then (if the children had bothered to count, they would have learned that it was every third time), the old Negro whipped his silver-tipped cane around behind him, fast and without warning, and the children jumped and dodged and laughed hysterically, though some were caught about the legs, the sound a loud and terrible *whack*. They ran to their friends again and rubbed at the painful welts, laughing through their tears and keen to try their luck again.

'To your health, sir,' Bayman Quince Rotterdam said to Krüger. 'And to the soul of that poor horrible Negro, that he might suffer no more than one eternity, and possibly a half again.'

They were drinking *sangaree*: Madeira wine, sugar, nutmeg and water. It was still sometime before midday. Krüger had bought a second carafe, which was already more than two-thirds gone. And all of it straight to his head.

'Drink, good sir, drink!' Bayman Quince Rotterdam said. 'For we are in mourning and this be a wake!'

He swung the cane behind him again and caught one of the children across the thigh.

'Many years ago, good sir,' he said, 'my beloved owner sailed me to Europe and paraded my esteemed self before the princes and dukes, the princesses and duchesses, and finally before the King of Holland himself. I was celebrated for my *intelligence* and indeed I was awarded a medal for my *comportment*. They placed a broad orange sash of the purest, finest silk over my head, with a clasp of solid silver, set with blue and red gemstones and a small diamond. Yes, sir, celebrated for my *bearing*. My beloved owner allowed me my honours; they be earned fairly, he said. But here, upon our return, among this filth and deception and criminal degeneracy, there was no respect to be found. My treasures were taken from me! Stolen by a black devil, my due and glory denied, and now not a single citizen believe my true self. But you believe me, good sir, when I say I be praying his soul, that damn thieving Negro whomsoever he be, that he suffer slow, excruciating torments. And that mean and treacherous Mr Hendrik, oh, it wasn't him, but he knew who done it and refused to tell. Refused me!' He drank down his glass of *sangaree* and poured the remainder from the carafe. 'Everything here be rotten, yes! Be rotten to the bone and to the marrow.'

Krüger put a coin on the table and motioned to the proprietor. 'Mr Hendrik said you might help me find his sister,' he said.

'Did he now?'

Krüger put a second coin on the table.

'Young Josephine, she shone and now she gone,' Bayman Quince Rotterman said. 'Stolen and sold and sent to the east.' He pointed with his cane over Krüger's shoulder. 'Stolen and sold to live with French beasts!'

'I don't understand.'

'Bonis burn down the plantation, good sir. Murder the captain, Captain van der Velde, murder the wife and murder the daughters, true. They strung the captain up in a tree. Took his hands. Took Josephine, took everything.'

Krüger felt a wave of weariness.

The old Negro smiled, than sang, '*Rotten brothers, rotten sisters, no manners, no! Every one you see, and everywhere you go!*'

The children ran up and repeated the song behind him; Bayman Quince Rotterdam swung his cane back with a smirk, then licked his lips.

'Do you know where she is?' Krüger said.

'Oh, good sir, I know all! Yes, all there is to know I know!'

The old Negro poured the remaining *sangaree* into a flask. They left the tavern and he led Krüger out of town, further up the river.

'It's going to rain,' he said, striding with his cane. 'A good 'un storm!'

They walked and walked, along the river, through the bends and bushes. Finally a grassy bank, Negroes and naked Indians washing at the water's edge, and there were others cleaning fish and eels that were heaped upon the grass and inside the canoes. The river was dark green and the branches of dead trees reached up out of the water. Bayman Quince Rotterdam approached a man and they shook hands. There was a young boy beside him, holding a wooden spear for fishing.

'Your son has grown, Dante,' Bayman Quince Rotterdam said.

'And I be shrunken.'

The boy had long eyelashes, fine-boned cheeks and slender shoulders, light-skinned like his father. His name was Aranjo.

'Can you take this man to Guyane?' Bayman Quince Rotterdam asked. 'He searches for Mr Hendrik's sister.'

Dante looked at Krüger with no expression, then down at his son. He knew about all that had happened at Captain van der Velde's plantation.

'What if she is not there?' Dante replied.

'Then she is not there,' Krüger said. 'But you'll be paid.'

Dante nodded. 'When do you wish to go?'

LORD OLDHAM FALLS ASLEEP

The fire warmed the backs of Claus von Rolt's legs. He'd gone to stand there in order to stay awake. Lord Oldham had been talking about shortages of men for the navy, about another recruitment push through the northern villages and west to Whitehaven, about the Admiralty's hope for five thousand more men.

'Deserters, that's the bloody problem!' he said. 'Bloody cowards.'

It was just the two of them. The room was close, the candle-light soft, the cognac glowed in each man's cheeks and chests. And all the time the Englishman talked, the shrunken head had been calling Rolt from the cabinet. He couldn't think about anything else.

'We'll round 'em up though,' Lord Oldham said conclusively.

A clock chimed somewhere in the house. Rolt realised he hadn't been listening; that in fact he'd closed his eyes for a moment and almost fallen asleep, standing up in front of the fire. He opened his eyes, embarrassed, but it didn't matter. Lord Oldham had dropped chin to chest and was snoring lightly in his deep chair.

Rolt finished his cognac. He waited a little while, but Lord Oldham didn't stir. He turned and put the glass down on the mantelpiece. He was wide awake now.

He went over to the cabinet and opened the glass door (a faint, hollow shudder). He unhooked the plaited leather cord and took the shrunken head out. He cradled it in his palm, surprised at the dense weight. The hair, when he touched it, was coarse and dry and not like hair at all. Rolt carefully put his finger to the blackened skin of its sunken cheeks too, its forehead, the shrivelled, grotesque lips and swollen eyes. The head seemed to be merely asleep, just like Lord Oldham.

Rolt took a white silk handkerchief from his pocket and shook out the folds. He wrapped the shrunken head there and then slipped it into his pocket. He carefully closed the cabinet door.

The maid helped him with his coat.

'Goodnight, sir,' she said and opened the front door.

Rolt smiled and nodded. 'Lord Oldham may need a blanket,' he said and stepped outside. The cold air was a shock. As he began to walk, his heart was beating fast.

SWIFTWING

James Noble was well and truly done with King and Country.

At twenty-two, he was still no bigger than he'd been at thirteen. He had glossy black hair and coal eyes too, and a good nose until the regiment champ broke it in a betting bout (he was still a touch wobbly at times, weeks later).

All James Noble needed was somebody to help him with the boat.

Harris wouldn't do it—he was desperate for family and home (up north on the Kentish coast)—and, besides, it made more sense to take the Prussian, who'd surely be wanting to head that way, across the Channel.

They fixed it all for the same night. Easy enough, with Harris in the guardhouse and the keys on a hook.

Nobody spoke. They took the keys and let Johannes Meyer out of his cell. They opened the front door and ran for the trees. Simple as that.

'Ten pounds says you'll see Old Bailey before me,' James Noble said when they'd made it to cover.

'Sure.' Harris smiled. 'But how would you ever know?'

A moment later, he was gone.

Noble turned to Johannes. There was a wrenching feeling in his guts. He hadn't expected it. 'We go this way,' he said.

There was a fine drizzle falling and the ground was soft and the grass slapped wetly against their boots as they ran, crouching, though the darkness. They were headed down to a cove about a mile along the coast. When they got there, Noble revealed a small round boat, hidden underneath branches. He saw the dubious look on Johannes Meyer's face.

'It's just a paddle to the real boat, son. Don't panic. It'll get us there.'

Johannes climbed in first and then James Noble pushed off and jumped in behind, almost tipping them over. He settled on his knees and began to paddle, but the coracle turned like a wheel over the water, no keel, and the two of them aboard like children on a fairytale leaf. It was woven of wicker and stank of brine and fish guts and everything was wet and slimy with dew. Neither man was particularly fond of the sea, and less so now.

'Use your hands,' Noble said. 'We'll get there quicker.'

The lugger was about a quarter-mile off the coast. First they had to swing around a ragged finger of rock to get its bearing. Shapes appeared there, dark stone skulls against the night sky. They could hear the soft rhythmic hiss of the tide as it spread and sank into the gravel and shell scree of the beach.

'Keep her straight,' Noble said. 'Haste, my friend!'

They paddled steadily and the sea lapped at them and soon the dawn crept into the horizon. The clouded sky turned pale orange and pink.

'It's grand, isn't it?' Noble said, pointing at the sunrise. 'That way, my good man, into the light!'

Johannes Meyer's hands were numb and he was cold and uncertain.

They paddled, spun about, seemed to go nowhere. Maybe an hour passed and then a fog rolled in. Before it settled completely, Noble cried out, 'There!'

She'd been a *chasse-marée* once upon a time, smuggling wool to the French; now she hauled mackerel as a lowly fishing lugger. *Swiftwing*. Ghostly and beautiful in the morning light. Noble smacked Johannes on the shoulder. Both men were grinning with relief.

MOSES

The boards of the guillotine were slicked with blood. The doctor moved quickly; there was no time to lose. He went to his knees beside the basket, reached in and turned the head around so that he was staring at the man's face.

Breathing fast, Dr Antoine Girodet leaned the severed head against the side of the basket, cursing himself now for not having thought to bring something—a rolled-up towel or a block of wood—to stop it from falling over. But he managed to fix the head at an angle, then instantly let go, aware that he'd already contaminated the experiment (too late!).

Girodet gripped the sides of the basket, ignoring the warm blood seeping into the knees of his pants.

'Moses!' the doctor said. 'Moses!'

The eyelids seemed to flicker, but remained closed. It was baking hot in the courtyard and the sun was directly above.

'Four seconds,' Christophe Bergerard said, standing over Girodet's shoulder, a watch ticking in the palm of his hand. This was the second experiment he'd been involved with since agreeing to the doctor's offer and terms of employment. The first had yielded no science to record.

'Moses!' Girodet said again, wanting to shake the basket with frustration but managing to restrain himself. It had taken bribes and bargaining (food, liquor, women), threats and violence, finally the promise of setting his wife and children free to convince the Negro to cooperate. And now he was holding out!

'I still have your children!' Girodet said. 'Can you hear me, Moses? Your wife and your children!'

'Seven seconds,' Bergerard said.

Girodet leaned in, agonised, desperately willing the Negro's head to give him a sign, a twitch of the cheek or of the lips, if not the eyes blinking as they had agreed to. Anything! But quickly, by Christ, for the window was closing rapidly.

Ten to twenty seconds, post-decapitation, Jacques de Dieu had estimated, *until life slipped the body entire.*

'Do it, Moses! Tell me!'

Bergerard said, 'Ten seconds.'

Girodet snapped, gave in to his anger and slapped the severed head across the cheek. It rolled around in the bottom of the basket. Then the doctor reached in and gripped the Negro by his ears, picked up the head and stood and held it in front of him.

'Hear me, Moses!' he said.

'Fifteen seconds.'

'Hear me!'

And then, by God, the eyelids opened.

Girodet almost dropped the head from shock. He saw the pupils dilate. He felt a great trembling through his body. It had happened. The slave Moses had opened his eyes.

'If you can hear me, Moses,' the doctor said, 'blink!'

The eyes blinked once, slow as a drunkard's.

Girodet said, 'How many children have you sired, Moses?'

The eyes closed, but then stayed closed as the seconds ticked ... two ... three ... then slowly, separately, each gluey lid opened on a bloodshot eye. There seemed much effort behind it, much will.

'Yes!' Girodet said. 'How many children do you have? Blink the number, Moses! Blink it!'

Once.

Twice.

'Yes! How many?'

The eyelids closed.

Then nothing.

Girodet waited.

But it was over.

After a moment, he dropped the head back into the basket. '*Merde*,' he said. Moses had five children.

He turned to Bergerard. 'Time?'

'Twenty-two seconds,' Bergerard said.

'You saw it?'

'Everything.'

Christophe Bergerard handed the doctor a rag to wipe his bloody hands.

'Well,' Girodet said. 'Not too bad.'

'When do you want to try again?' There was another slave locked up in the washhouse.

'Tomorrow,' Girodet said. The beautiful mulatto girl was waiting for him. 'Will you write it all up for me, Christophe?'

'Of course.'

'There will be more arriving on Thursday with the agent, too. If he can get through, we won't be short.'

'I'll take care of it.'

Dr Antoine Girodet left the courtyard. He would have to wash up before he saw Josephine.

Bergerard looked down at the head in the basket. One eye had opened again. It was fixed on him but saw right through Bergerard, somewhere far beyond.

'Barbu!' he called out.

The old slave ran over with two others. They collected the head and body of Moses, then set to cleaning down the bloody guillotine with brooms and buckets of water.

ALONE

A young Portuguese corporal and an old Creole man with a mule and wagon came to escort Elisabeth to the Hôtel de la République, right in the centre of town. Christophe had decided to remain with the doctor.

'What else can I do with the général gone?' he said. 'I have no money or work and Girodet has offered me both.'

'He guillotines slaves.'

'For science.'

Elisabeth von Hoffmann said nothing. She kissed the général's aide-de-camp on the cheek. 'Be careful, Christophe.' Then she climbed up into the wagon and sat beside the old

Creole man (who smelled of fish), relieved to be leaving Girodet and his disconcerting hospitality behind.

They moved off. The day was already hot and humid. Every day was the same, every day was hot and humid; every day the heat pressed down and the buildings and trees in Cayenne shimmered in the light. As the sun rose, the world slowed and sank and the day took twice as long to pass.

The wagon swayed and rocked over the uneven road.

The young Portuguese corporal led them on his small brown horse and twice he turned his head and smiled at Elisabeth. After a time, he let the wagon come up alongside him.

He looked over to Elisabeth and touched his hat. 'If you will permit me, Mademoiselle?'

Elisabeth nodded. The young corporal's face was flushed and shiny with sweat.

'They have taken the Général Fourés to Rio de Janeiro,' he said. 'Please do not say that I have told you this.'

'Why have they taken him there?' Elisabeth had been to see endless officials but nobody had told her a thing.

The young corporal shrugged. 'I do not know. I am sorry.'

He rode the horse back up to lead the wagon again. Children ran across the road, dogs sniffed and weaved, there were soldiers on foot in pairs, Portuguese, a few English. Negro women balanced bundles on their heads, hips swaying like palms.

At the hotel, the young corporal helped Elisabeth down and then he and the old man carried her luggage to the room.

'My name is Duarte dos Santos,' he said at the door. 'Please, Mademoiselle, if you need my help, you must ask. Anything.'

'Thank you, Duarte,' Elisabeth said. She liked the feeling of his name as she spoke it. 'You are very kind.'

Corporal Duarte dos Santos bowed and walked off. His boots echoed down the stairs. He hoped, deep in his heart, that she would indeed call upon him.

Elisabeth closed the door and turned to the empty room. Part of her felt an overwhelming sense of loneliness, of having been abandoned. She could barely grasp in her mind everything that had happened, the distance she'd come. But another part of her trembled with nervous excitement.

She went downstairs and ordered hot water for a bath, and then she opened all the windows and shutters in her room, let the heat pour in.

EXTRACTS FROM THE RECORDS OF
THE BEXHILL COURT MARTIAL
13 SEPTEMBER 1810

(1) Testimony of Charles William Talbert, pilot of His Majesty's cutter *Arrowhead*: 'They had her mizzen for a foresail and the foresail out for a main and you'd have caught more air in a coat if you'd've known what you were doing, Your Honour.'

(2) Testimony of George Boulton, owner of *Swiftwing*, in pursuit of the stolen craft aboard His Majesty's cutter *Arrowhead*:

'When the fog came in we thought, well, that's it, we'll never catch up now, not with the cover and then the night coming and the wind in the right direction. But we sailed out for a look in the morning and the fog blew off quick like. She'd basically drifted down the coast, and when we got to her, she was sitting like a log on the water and one of 'em was splashing an oar around.'

Lieutenant-Colonel J.W.R. Pike for the Prosecution: 'How far had she sailed?'

Boulton: 'Oh, about six or seven miles off the Hythe head. But to be perfectly accurate, sir, there were no sailing about it.'

(3) Lieutenant-Colonel J.W.R. Pike for the Prosecution, questioning Sergeant Edward Tennant, who'd been aboard His Majesty's cutter *Arrowhead* in pursuit of the two deserters from the 2nd Light Battalion of the King's German Legion: 'It has been claimed, Sergeant Tennant, that the two accused called out, "France! France!" in an excited manner and with their arms waving when His Majesty's cutter *Arrowhead* became visible to them after the fog lifted. Is this correct?'

Sergeant Edward Tennant: 'Yes, that is correct, sir.'

Lieutenant-Colonel J.W.R. Pike: 'How did you interpret their actions?'

Sergeant Edward Tennant: 'They thought we were French, sir. They believed they'd made it across the Channel and reached the coast of France.'

Lieutenant-Colonel J.W.R. Pike: 'Were they fearful or gleeful?'

Sergeant Edward Tennant: 'I would say they were gleeful, sir.'

Lieutenant-Colonel J.W.R. Pike, addressing the Judge Advocate: 'I understand this as no less than an act of treason. I submit the prisoners should be hung until dead as in accordance with the law.'

(4) Lieutenant E.P. King Carr for the Defence: 'I beg the court to bear in mind that though clearly these two men are guilty of absconding, their motivations were never treasonous. Private Noble was escaping extreme abuse at the hands of one Lieutenant Schneppen of the King's German Legion, who at this moment is conveniently on leave and could not appear before this court, and who has, I wish to state for the record, other charges pending against him. And Private Meyer, a Prussian ally who'd previously been forced into servitude with the French, who escaped and heroically served our king at Walcheren, was merely trying to get back home in order to help overthrow the French occupation of his own country.'

(5) Judge Advocate the Honourable E.H. Ampleforth: 'Based upon the evidence presented this day, I am inclined to agree with the Defence that the defendants were not intending to desert for the purposes of joining or fraternising with the enemy. However, there is no question of their intent to desert from the ranks of the King's German Legion, 2nd Light

Battalion, or of their wanton theft of the lugger *Swiftwing* during the attempt to do so. Therefore, I sentence Private James Francis Noble to transportation and fourteen years' penal servitude in His Majesty's colony of New South Wales, and Private Johannes Meyer to transportation and penal servitude for the term of his natural life in His Majesty's colony of New South Wales.'

BOOK VI

DIVORCE

The conqueror of Europe couldn't bring himself to do it (though he wanted it done and knew that it was inevitable), so he asked Hortense to speak to her mother, and then he asked Eugène, but Josephine's children said they'd not be party to it. He asked the archchancellor, who'd wrung his hands and pleaded to be spared the terrible task, and then he asked others too, but each had declined in turn, no matter the threats or promises.

Fontainebleau became miserable and oppressive, the whole situation exceedingly unpleasant, and the Emperor became volatile and raged unpredictably, more so than usual.

To everyone's great relief, the Duc d'Otrante accepted the burden.

On the designated day, in Bonaparte's study (where he'd been left alone to prepare), the ageing duke had a glass of the Emperor's brandy and fixed his clothes in the mirror. Then he had another brandy and two more after that, and then, finally, strode across to Josephine's chambers.

Graceful as ever, she answered the door and let him inside. The Duc d'Otrante cleared his throat and told the Empress that divorce was unavoidable and of utmost necessity in order for the Emperor to secure a dynasty with legitimate heirs.

'It is for France that he sacrifices himself, my Empress,' he said, exactly as he'd been instructed. 'For France.'

Josephine turned from the fireplace. She knew Napoleon's sentimental claptrap when she heard it, even via another's voice.

'Is that what you believe?'

The Duc d'Otrante blushed.

Josephine saw the old man's unease and felt pity for him. She understood how impossible it was to be oneself when tasked by Bonaparte.

'It is all right,' she said.

There was a noise in the next room. They both heard it and knew instantly that it was Bonaparte, listening at the connecting door.

Josephine raised her voice, managed to hold it from breaking, 'For France! But it is me he throws on the pyre.'

The divorce took place in the throne room of the Palais des Tuileries. Inside, it was dark and gloomy as a church. Napoleon sat solemn and lost to his thoughts, flanked by Maréchal Murat on the left, Eugène on his right. He'd just spoken ('God only knows how much this has cost my heart') and signed the act of annulment.

The Empress, dressed in white, stood with her daughter Hortense before the table draped in rich green velvet, where the Duc d'Otrante held the divorce act that now awaited her signature. The Bonaparte family sat in the spectator chairs behind her ('Good riddance,' Bonaparte's sister, Pauline, had whispered) along with the maréchals, Bessières and Ney, and there was Talleyrand too, of course, and a few other minor officials. Josephine could feel their eyes upon her as she signed the act. And then it was done.

Later, alone together in Bonaparte's chambers, they held each other.

'Be brave,' he said. 'I will always be your friend.'

He left her Malmaison. She would be free to retain her title and all her jewels and would be assured an annual allowance of some three million francs. He would honour all her debts. Her Paris residence would be at the Palais de l'Élysée.

But there were demands, too.

Josephine was to withdraw from public life and desist from scandalous behaviour. She would receive no special treatment, and should she be invited to an official event where her former husband was in attendance (particularly if in attendance with his new wife) she was not to expect acknowledgement from him of any kind, they were not to speak with one another and she was *never* to approach him.

'I understand,' Josephine said.

A few days later she left Paris for Malmaison, accompanied by her daughter, her household staff and her parrot. Once she'd settled in again, Bonaparte came to visit. They held hands and strolled through the beautiful gardens in the mist. There were kisses too, affectionate, brother-and-sisterly, on the cheek. 'I am greatly saddened,' the Emperor admitted. He visited Josephine three days in a row.

His sadness didn't last. On the fourth day he left and returned to Paris.

Bonaparte's new royal wife was on her way from Austria. Nineteen-year-old Marie-Louise, daughter of the Emperor Francis and great-niece of the dead queen, Marie Antoinette. There was work to be done in producing an heir.

ON THE RIVER COTTICA

Dante paddled from the rear of the canoe, while his boy Aranjo kneeled up in the nose and kept an eye out for sunken trees and caiman. Krüger sat in the middle, mute with heat and pressed by the wet, tangled lushness bearing over him, the cacophony of birdcalls and screaming monkeys and the air alive with insects. The smell of mud rot in the riverbanks, the relentless hot green breath of the forest.

His soft, sodden, bread-white body sweated and suffered.

They'd been on the river for days. The last time Dante had spoken, he'd told Krüger to remove his boots.

'Easy for feet to die,' he'd said.

But Krüger was too afraid to take his boots off.

There was still a long way to go. They would paddle the river all the way to Devil's Harwar, then further to Barbacoeba and Casepoere, and then to the settlement of Jerusalem on the Cormoetibo Creek. Depending on the rains, they'd either take the Wana Creek to the River Marawina and so to the border or, if there was flooding, make their way on foot through the forest. And all of it depending on the rebels, too; so far, they hadn't seen any.

When Dante spoke for the second time since they'd entered the river (there wouldn't be a third time for another six days) he said, 'There,' and pointed to a rough clearing that began at a low riverbank on their left. 'Mr Hendrik,' he said. 'Home.'

'He was there?'

Dante nodded.

It was hard to believe. Everything was overgrown, almost completely hidden by vines and grass, bushes and young trees, but as the canoe came by, Krüger could just see the burnt-out remains of a few buildings. Then his eye was caught by piles of rusted iron, barrel bands, sluices and tools, their timber handles rotted away. He saw a sunken river barge in the mud near the bank and the rotted posts where the jetty had stood. But not much else. There were no paths anywhere, no traces of previous order. No rows of tamarind trees or European rosebushes, lime and lemon groves gone wild, nothing equal to what Mr Hendrik had described, to the vastness Krüger had imagined. He couldn't see hundreds of slaves, grand houses, outbuildings, double-storeyed distilleries, sugarcane fields stretching for miles, a river full of laden barges.

He never would have believed it, seeing this first. It was like waking from a vivid dream, and the disappointments of reality.

Dante and the boy paddled them by. The jaguars had long carried off Captain van der Velde's bones (his hands, which had been sold in Paramaribo, were lost now, too). All that remained was his Bible, in the sack by Krüger's foot, and some of the gold coins his electrical eels had earned, snug in the secret board sleeves.

And Josephine, maybe, somewhere up ahead.

CRUCIFIXION

The Indians sometimes came and stood on the riverbanks as they canoed by, appearing like ghosts out of the forest, but they hadn't seen any for some days now.

The river cut deeper into the forest floor. The trees were taller, looming, the sky was only a thin speckle of pale blue through the darkened treetops. Around them the forest was an even more tightly woven mass of lush green. Clouds of mosquitoes attacked them, flew into their ears, eyes, their mouths. The heat sapped Krüger day and night.

They paddled into a chasm of sheer rock. The river slowed and seemed to work against them, as though they were climbing uphill. Dante and Aranjo rested, the boy curling up to sleep, his father with the food sack in his lap. He'd killed and salted a howler monkey some miles back and now removed an arm from inside the hessian. Snapping off the hand at the wrist, he tapped Krüger on the shoulder and held it out to him. The Prussian looked at the raw skinless fingers and yellow fat, the knuckles, the strands of sinew hanging from the wrist, shook his head and turned away before he began to retch. It was exactly as a child's hand. He leaned over the side of the canoe and splashed water onto his face.

Dante frowned at him, threw the hand back into the sack and began to eat, gnawing at the thin meat of the howler monkey's forearm.

The river was very deep and cold and there was nowhere to climb out. The boy woke a little while later and again he and his father stroked their paddles through the water.

Krüger dozed; over hours, days, weeks, he had no idea. When he opened his eyes, everything was different and yet always the same. Time didn't pass but seemed to hover over them like a cloud, like mist, changing shape imperceptibly.

Ten miles on, he woke to the roar of water. Dante pointed ahead, then slapped the side of the canoe, showed Krüger how to grip it. 'Hold good!' he said. His face was drawn tight, his eyes wide and awake, brow ridged.

A few times they crashed and scraped against the walls of rock. Dante and the boy had to use the paddles to get them away, careful not to push too hard, capsize the canoe. Then, in a moment, they hit the rapids with a shock. The force of the river was immense, the noise unbelievable.

Dante dug his paddle in hard, reached deep into the twisting water and dragged, leaning back with the handle against his chest. In the nose, his boy Aranjo did the same. The canoe almost smashed into a knuckle of rock but scraped over the top and righted itself, regained its line through the current. Father and son began to paddle as fast as they could, Dante yelling, his voice drowned by the roar and hissing foam.

The canoe rushed down terrifying slopes of cold muscled water. Still Dante shouted through the bursting spray, but Krüger couldn't understand a thing he said. Then the canoe suddenly fell away beneath them and for a moment everything hung in the air. They smacked the water again, the canoe was twisted and churned by the mad current; they barely managed to stay afloat. Dante and the boy paddled and tried to hold the river off, but then they hit another drop and this time it seemed to go on forever.

The canoe tipped. Krüger flew through the air. There was a momentary sensation of weightlessness, then a hard, jarring crash that went right through his spine. The river exploded around him, reared up, fell away and splashed high, white-capped, roiled and roared. The river was alive, animal. He realised with terror that he was in the water and there was nothing below his feet.

The current had him by the boots and the river turned him over and over and Krüger thrashed his arms and legs in unthinking fear. Nothing happened except that he was sucked down into the river; nothing happened except that he gasped and kicked in terror and then the water was over his head and he clamped his mouth shut and held his breath.

The light dimmed. It was green, silted light, and he looked down deeper and under him the water was brown, and there were dark shadow shapes in it, too. Krüger tried his arms and legs again but they were so heavy. The river pummelled his body and dragged him lower and lower into its depths.

Ahead of him, a form took shape in the water. When he saw it clearer, Krüger thrust out again in panic. Tilted against a ledge of rock was a wooden cross. There was an Indian tied to its beams. His long hair waved in the water. His body was bloated and the skin was blue-white and there were dark cancerous bruises spreading from the armpits. There were nails in his wrists and in his feet. The Indian's eyes were open, but there were no eyes there, only rough holes, puckered and trailing thin veins and strands of pale flesh.

Krüger kicked desperately with his legs. His feet caught the ledge of rock where the cross was wedged and he pushed up off it, eyes on the light above him, reaching for it, the light.

Oh God.

He let go his last burning breath.

CURADO AND MARTA

After his arrest, Général Fourés was transferred to the *São Jorge* and then sailed to Rio de Janeiro.

The weather was clear, calm, and the Portuguese were respectful and attentive. In truth, they were in awe of his having served Bonaparte, having been in the man's presence, having heard his voice and done his bidding. They were only one link away in the human chain (one!) from the greatest military leader since Alexander. Such proximity to fame was irresistible. They looked at Fourés as though Bonaparte might have been right there, standing just over his shoulder. They imagined them together, serious and plotting over maps in Bonaparte's field tent, then laughing and sitting down to dinner: cognac and roast chicken.

The général could see all this. He was happy to inflate so few actual occasions to many. (It was time Bonaparte paid his due.)

In Rio de Janeiro, he was placed under house arrest on the top floor of a three-storey house not far from the monastery of Morro de São Bento. It was sparsely furnished but clean. The two small windows were barred, but there was a nice view of the harbour between the iron. Watching the ships come and go helped pass some of the hours. He was fed in the morning (bread, a small piece of cheese, a bowl of sweet milky coffee, brandy) and then again in the evening (black beans, rice, sometimes a piece of roast pork, bread, wine) and there was always a basket of fruit (bananas, mango, papaya and avocado; he gorged on the fruit, stunned by the gushing sweetness, the ecstasy of the taste). There was fresh water to wash with, even soap that smelled of lemons. And soon there was the field marshal, too, who helped the days pass quickly and more comfortably.

Joaquim Xavier Curado, Count of São João das Duas Barras, was a thin man with sharp cheekbones and a fine nose, sad hazel eyes and hair gone completely white. His boots were tall, right up to his knees, and polished to an extreme shine. He wore spurs with dainty rowels that sounded out a light *ching* like sleigh bells when he walked. Of Bonaparte, he couldn't hear enough.

'They say he only sleeps two hours a day?'

'He doesn't sleep at all,' Fourés said.

'And a week in the saddle, without stepping down?'

'Even now he rides his horse through the halls of Versailles and pisses from the stirrups.'

'You mock me, Général!'

'I have seen it all with my own eyes.'

Curado always brought tobacco and brandy, and together they sat and talked through the evening heat. Fourés was grateful; afterwards, it was always easier for him to fall asleep, a little drunk and distracted from his predicament and loneliness.

Soon enough they became friends and spoke freely to one another, enjoying the opportunity to talk of things outside the contaminations of war, politics and God, temporary though it was. Sundays and Wednesdays. The first few months went by swiftly, thanks to the field marshal.

One night, Curado said, 'I've tried, Général, to have your circumstances reconsidered, but our Prince Regent remains stubborn. He is still extremely annoyed with Bonaparte for having forced his retreat from Lisbon. And as you are the Emperor's closest and highest representative to hand . . .'

'We are like brothers.'

'For now, you must continue to endure.' Curado stood and went to the window. He called out for his adjutant, who immediately came in through the door.

'There,' Curado said, pointing to the table.

'Yes, Field Marshal.'

The adjutant began to remove items from a sack. There were bottles of wine, brandy, champagne, a small, stoppered earthenware jug of herbal digestive, tobacco, sugar and cured bacon. The adjutant left the room again and then came back with a pile of folded clothes: trousers, shirts, underwear, socks. Also, a new pair of Portuguese boots.

'That is all,' the field marshal said.

The young adjutant left the room and closed the door behind him.

Curado came over, rapped his knuckles twice against the tabletop. 'So. I will be gone for a time.'

'War?'

'Yes, a small one,' Curado said. 'Across the Rio de la Plata. The Spanish are annoying the Prince Regent, too.'

'He is easily annoyed?'

'He is a spoilt child and thus men must die.'

'Then I wish you good fortune and look forward to your return.' Fourés pointed to the food and clothes. 'And thank you.'

'There is one other gift, Général, that I wish to make,' Curado said. 'I hope you will not take offence.'

She came the next evening, a young Pataxó Indian girl from the Bahia. The old man who swept the room and emptied the slop bucket led her through the door, her delicate wrist in his dry, arthritic hand. She was dark brown and small and very beautiful, with long shining black hair and round hips. She wore a simple white cotton dress, barefoot, and her ankles were ringed in bracelets of plaited leather and colourful stones, as were her wrists. There was a large wooden crucifix hanging from her neck.

'Marta,' the old man said and left. The door closed and the bolt snapped.

'Marta,' the général said.

The young Indian girl smiled. She walked over and stood by the bed, reached down for the hem of her dress and then pulled it up over her head. She dropped it to the floor. The candlelight flickered as she turned and slid naked inside the single white sheet.

Général Fourés sat at the table and sipped Curado's brandy. That first night he sat and drank and watched Marta until she fell asleep.

HULK

'Floatin' Sodoms,' the man next to him said. 'You'd best beware and never mind bendin' down for the thing you dropped.'

Johannes Meyer tried not to breathe as the man leaned across and laughed into his ear.

The prisoners were assembled on the quarterdeck. The captain had come to watch while the guards went from man to man and collected money, rings, necklaces, bracelets, buttons, keepsakes, anything in their possession. They patted down pockets and checked the linings of coats and the hems of shirts and trousers. They grabbed jaws and squeezed them open and looked inside, sometimes ran a grimy finger under the tongue and around the gums. Men retched and spat on the deck.

'It's just for safekeeping, son,' the guards would say, as they pulled a gold tooth with rusty pliers or a silver ring from the prisoner's finger. 'Don't fret none. We'll look after it for you.'

'In the ship's hold!'

'In the Hulk Workers' Benevolent Fund!'

'Aye!'

Coats were confiscated too, decent pairs of shoes, any shirts or pants well tailored and of good material, all swapped for the ragged, filthy hulk uniform.

A tidy profit on the hulks, oh yes, split half to the captain and the rest distributed according to rank among the guards.

They finished gathering the haul. Leg irons dragged across the deck, just heavy enough to drown a man, should he think of jumping into the Thames. The prisoners were pushed and hustled below into the stifling decks, paired off into the berths. The timbers reeked, greasy and dark, the air was dead.

'Hot as a whore's arsehole!'

She'd been a French warship once, eighty guns in her glory, but the cannons had long been smelted into English rivets and nails. Just a rotten box now, chocked with three hundred souls, moored slack and iron-chained in a line of other former glories. The stench enough in each, they said, to almost keep the rats away.

Men came and went and died. Johannes Meyer waited, survived.

THE MAN WHO CAME OUT OF THE SEA

There were almost a dozen Portuguese officers pursuing Elisabeth von Hoffmann, offering sanctuary in the grand houses they'd requisitioned from the French in Cayenne.

It is not good for one so young to live alone, they said.

And, they said, I will honour you.

They sent large bouquets of tropical flowers to her room at the Hôtel de la République, and gifts of expensive perfumes and dresses, even pages of original verse. Elisabeth declined their invitations and kept everything but the poetry.

As the hottest months of the year brewed the coming storms, so the competitiveness of the officers grew more intense with each of Elisabeth's refusals. Her unattainability and its breaching became nothing less than a test of Portuguese manhood itself. She was a distraction from their boredom and their inglorious military careers (deep down, the officers all knew they'd been assigned to a backwater). They argued and threatened and fought one another in drunken duels. Only one man was ever seriously injured.

Mostly, the situation angered Elisabeth. For weeks and then months she'd begged the Portuguese authorities for news of the général, but they'd refused to tell her a thing ('You are not his wife, Mademoiselle'). She asked the colony's deposed French officers and former administrators to help ('But we are powerless!') and the général's aide-de-camp, Christophe Bergerard, seemed to have disappeared without trace. Desperate, Elisabeth even met with one of her ridiculous suitors (an excruciating dinner, a carriage ride through Cayenne, the man preening like a duke) in the hope he might trade news for her attentions, but discovered only that the man was a goat and she'd slapped him as hard as she could and stepped out of the carriage and walked back to her hotel.

Elisabeth understood she was vulnerable, and she was angry at the feeling too, at her status, and because there was nothing she could do but wait.

She made friends with some of the French wives in Cayenne, who tolerated her, on occasion. Every Tuesday, Thursday and Saturday she went to the market in the cooler early mornings, bought exotic fruit to try. In the afternoon, torpor. She read novels and fell asleep for an hour or two, then later bathed in the dark. She took long walks on the beach and sat on the sand and watched the sea.

One day she saw a naked man walk out of the waves.

His skin was very brown and his long dark hair was slicked back over his head. Water ran off his body and glinted in the sun. He was down a little way from where she sat in the hot dunes, and he'd appeared so suddenly that now she was stunned and didn't know what to do. Elisabeth twitched to move, but knew if she stood up the man would certainly see her. The truth was, whether she moved or not, any moment now he'd see her anyway.

The man, dripping, strode to a pile of clothes on the beach. He turned to look back at the water, put his hands on his hips, stood in the sea breeze drying off. After a while he picked up a white shirt and slipped it over his head, then pulled on a pair of breeches. He sat down and brushed the sand from his feet.

Elisabeth squinted through the glare. Maybe he wouldn't see her after all.

When the man stood again, he gathered up a coat and draped it over his arm, bent down for his boots. Then he looked over at Elisabeth and smiled and bowed his head. He began walking away slowly down the beach.

BEHIND CLOSED DOORS

Claus von Rolt had a small mahogany box made for the shrunken head. The wood was engraved in old Celtic patterns and inside it was lined with cushioned black velvet. Fine silver hinges and clasps attached the lid, and there was a delicate filigreed lock and key, the small key a jewel, just like the keys on music boxes. It had cost him a lot of money.

Each time he opened the box, it was with great anticipation, and the thrill of seeing the head never diminished, in fact only intensified. Opening the box was like lifting the lid on a holy relic, once possessed by bishops and kings, Alexander the Great, Kublai Khan, Caesar.

To wear the head in public was an incredible feeling, but it bulged under his clothing and looked strange. Only a coat and scarf hid its presence; unfortunately, the English weather had turned unseasonably mild.

At night, Rolt undressed and wore it naked through his rented rooms.

He'd run through the rooms as fast and silently as he could on the balls of his feet, run until he began to sweat, until he collapsed on the cold floor, exhilarated. He'd rest a moment, do it again, sometimes four, five times, the head around his neck, running.

He longed to run outside in the open, in the starred dark and under the sun, across a field and through the desert, streaming between the trees of a dense green forest. A warrior running.

Claus von Rolt ran through his rented rooms and imagined himself in new lands and on endless grass plains, running, faster, his chest heaving. In the mirrors of his rented rooms, he'd pause and look and be unable to see himself at all.

By the end of the month, he'd booked passage on an English ship, the convict transport *Guildford*, bound for New South Wales.

LONDON — CANARY ISLANDS — RIO DE JANEIRO — CAPE TOWN — PORT JACKSON

The prisoners were given lighter leg irons and their last rancid rations, and then they were ferried off the hulk. None of them received any of their possessions back.

Carted by bony bullock teams to the London docks, they were unloaded under guard and then long-boated again, over to where their ship waited at anchor. A few women had gathered and called out to their husbands. They cried bitterly and held up their children. Some of the women spat on the guards. They were pushed away and sworn at. Scuffles broke out and the women scratched at the guards' faces.

'Bastards! Scum!'

'You give it to 'em, darlin'!'

'Fuckers!'

The sky was low and overcast. The Thames was still, flat and briny and the pebbly shoreline was fish-gutted and strewn with rotting seaweed, but Johannes Meyer was grateful to breathe the open air in deeply.

One by one for the next few hours, two hundred male convicts scaled the salt-wet rope ladders slack against the hull of the *Guildford*, up onto the deck. Bewildered and exhausted and weak, they took small shuffling steps in their leg irons as they were herded into lines and accounted for. Marked off the list, they hobbled over to a hatch in the deck and climbed down into the hold. It was hot and the same prison hulk stench was there too, though in truth, really, not so bad as that.

Down the ladder, again from light into dark.

'Get ya foot off me head!'

'Get ya 'ead off me foot!'

'Move it!'

Down the ladder, into the hold.

They rushed and wrestled for the berths nearer the hatchways. They fought, dominance and subservience re-established. The weakest would trade all sorts of favours down the line.

After some time, the heavy vibration of the anchor chain suddenly rumbled through the hull. Not a man moved, each one stock-still, sentences cut off in the middle, thoughts slashed, dropped dead. They listened.

The timbers boomed and the ship groaned, the bow dipped under the strain; the men stood braced. Above they could hear the sailors running and shouting now, and whistles blew and their bare feet drummed the deck and then, just like that, the *Guildford* came free and began to float. Every man's stomach lurched.

The shock broke. Those on the higher hold decks ran for the few fist-sized portholes cut into the hull for air, a final glimpse of England. Some wept quietly and others sang soft hymns, a few kneeled and prayed. Many sat silent on their berths and stared down into their hands. The youngest were defiant and whispered good riddance, the roughest swore oaths and vengeance.

The tide came in and Johannes Meyer heard the sails snap and flurry in the breeze. The ship swung to port and headed for the estuary, for the sea.

TALISMAN

The croaking of ten thousand frogs woke him. The swarming whir of a million mosquitoes, the screeching of bats as they burst in a black horde out of the treetops.

Krüger lay in the mud at the river's edge as the sun went down.

He dreamed of Hilde dying in Magdeburg, their cold room in the eaves. She was happy. She said, 'Send the doctor away.'

'No!' Krüger said.

'*Please*,' she said, but he couldn't look at her now and he was ashamed.

Dante tapped him on the shoulder, handed him a monkey hand, warm from roasting on a fire he'd lit on the floor of the room.

'For Hilde,' he said. 'She needs her strength.' Dante put the long, jointed thumb of the roasted monkey hand in his mouth, showed Krüger how to suck the meat off the bone. 'Like this,' he said, with a loud, slurping sound.

Krüger's nostrils filled with the putrid stink, his stomach clenched. He turned on his side and retched bile and river silt.

The Bible and the gold coins were gone, but Mr Hendrik's *obia* was still around his neck.

BOOK VII

THE KING OF ROME

Word eventually reached Bonaparte that Général de Brigade Michel François Fourés had been arrested by the Portuguese in Cayenne and imprisoned in Rio de Janeiro. The Emperor frowned upon hearing the news (he only vaguely recalled Fourés) and then shrugged.

'There is a Madame Fourés?'

'Yes, my Emperor,' the aide-de-camp said.

'A hero of France,' Bonaparte said, 'et cetera, et cetera. With great respect.' He leaned over the table and signed a blank piece of paper and handed it to the aide-de-camp. 'Be sure to maintain a formal but respectful tone.' The Emperor walked off. 'I will be with the King of Rome.'

When he arrived at his wife's chambers, he heard voices inside and paused at the door. He leaned in and listened, recognised the Duchesse de Montebello, *dame d'honneur* to the new Empress Marie-Louise.

He heard her say, 'I don't know, Empress.'

'Oh, she is very old now,' Marie-Louise said. 'All of her beauty, if she ever really had any, is gone.'

Bonaparte heard rustling and footsteps.

'And she is *fat*,' the Empress Marie-Louise said. 'She has ordered at least a dozen corsets, can you imagine? But they won't help her.'

'A dozen?'

'You cannot hide your origins behind whalebone.' (Marie-Louise had only just turned twenty and thought *I will never be fat*.)

'Her father owned a sugar plantation in Martinique.'

'And mine is just a king.' The Empress laughed sharply and when she stopped there was silence for a few moments. 'Show me the blue one again,' she said.

Bonaparte looked nervously up and down the hall. He wasn't sure if he should go in. Last night he'd been writing Josephine a letter and Marie-Louise had glimpsed the page over his shoulder.

'Again!' she'd said.

'I've told you, *ma chérie*. It's regarding her spending.'

'*Ma chérie, ma chérie!*' the Empress had shouted. 'My son is the King of Rome!'

In the next room, the boy woke and began to cry. Bonaparte put his ear right up to the door.

'Where is she now?' Marie-Louise said. 'The old woman my husband was so infatuated with?'

'At Malmaison, I believe, my Empress.'

'Of course she is. Strolling her magnificent gardens. With her *corsets.*'

Bonaparte heard a knock and then a door open in the room. The crying grew louder.

'The King of Rome, Empress,' a voice said. 'He is awake.'

'Yes,' Marie-Louise said. The child was wailing now. 'I am not *deaf.*'

ELECTRICITY

Alejandro Joaquin Montoya said, 'Why don't you come with me and see for yourself?'

'A hermit who lives in the forest?'

Montoya smiled. He had long eyelashes (the longest Elisabeth von Hoffmann had ever seen on a man) and deep brown eyes. He'd come all the way from Valdivia, in Chile, to find a monk they said had built a machine to make ice. Alejandro Joaquin Montoya had become wealthy from investing in rational minds, though it was a fact, he'd discovered, that the more untethered provided for the greater profit margins.

'It is on the River Comté,' Montoya said. 'A pleasant afternoon boat trip, Señorita.'

Elisabeth picked up her fan and cooled her neck, the flushed, sweating skin of her chest. They met often at the Hôtel de la République now, where Montoya was also staying. She liked his accent. Neither had ever mentioned the day on the beach.

'Caiman,' Elisabeth said.

'I will bring my guns.'

'Mosquitoes.'

'Camomile lotion,' Montoya said. 'The best. From Valdivia. The flowers grow in the mountains.'

Elisabeth looked out through the window, her eyes bright.

Montoya said, 'I have been told that during one of his experiments with electricity, the man burned every hair on his body and that it now refuses to grow back.'

'A hairless man of God who makes ice in the forest.'

Montoya leaned back in his chair. 'Eyelashes, eyebrows, the hair on his head, his arms, his legs, all of it gone.'

'I would hide in the forest, too.'

'I want to see what such a man looks like. Don't you?'

'There are mad men all over Cayenne,' Elisabeth said. 'You needn't go so far.'

'I am interested only in visionary men.'

In Caracas, Venezuela, Alejandro Joaquin Montoya had met a monk who showed him the cell of Brother Salinas. There was a sleeping pallet, a leather whip, three books (Feijóo's *Teatro crítico universal*, L'abbé Nollet's *Traité d'électricité* and Franklin's *Mémoires*) and an assemblage of glass jars, metal plates, discs, and various geological shards and rocks in the corner.

'Brother Salinas was discovered administrating electrical shocks to frogs and rats,' Montoya said. 'Then a day prior to his appearance before the bishop, he disappeared.'

Elisabeth shook her head. 'These visionaries,' she said. 'So unpredictable.'

Montoya caught the mocking tone, but wanted her to understand. 'Three books, a few bits and pieces, and the man had improvised electricity,' he said.

'And simultaneously offended God.'

Now Montoya smiled. 'Yes. That too.' He'd followed a trail of rumours and ever thinning luck to Cayenne. And now he'd met Elisabeth von Hoffmann, which wasn't so bad. Not by any means. 'Will you come?' he said.

Elisabeth closed and then opened her fan with a flick.

He waited for her to say yes. Montoya could sense that she would, but the situation was precariously balanced. He may have pushed too early. Her général was still in prison, he'd heard the story; and yet, how many times had he seen her sitting alone, her blue eyes sad and vacant? It had been a long time since her French général.

Jealousy spiked in him; Montoya frowned. Enough, he told himself. Best to keep quiet and add no more, let the scales settle with their weights in silence. But he drank her in with his eyes and knew there could never be any sating, that she would forever compel his desire and need, never fulfil it.

Elisabeth smiled, still gazing out the window. Then she turned to look at Montoya.

'It's true,' she said. 'I have never before met a hairless visionary who offends God with electricity. Maybe I should?'

HEATWAVE

Fifty-three days after sailing out of London, the *Guildford* dropped anchor in Rio de Janeiro and took on provisions. She remained in port for another six days, waiting for the arrival of the *General Graham*, in whose company she'd sail on to Cape Town.

It was tremendously hot, but Captain Johnson decided to keep the prisoners below decks.

'Better not to encourage them with views of land,' he said, eyes on the lush mountains that encircled the harbour. 'We'll give them a walk on deck once we're out to sea again.'

The sun was the whole sky. Intense tropical heat poured down onto the ship, enough to spoil the beef in the brine barrels, melt the pitch in the deck timbers. It dripped down, hot and scalding, onto the prisoners below.

'How it rains in hell!' the man shackled to Johannes Meyer said.

The prisoners rattled their irons in protest, called out profanities, but were ignored.

By the third day, to placate them, Captain Johnson had extra water rations and fresh fruit distributed ('I am not a cruel man,' he said).

The soldiers guarding the hatchways were overwhelmed with the incredible stench as the rations were handed out. Soon it was discovered that one of the prisoners was dead and had been for some time.

Nobody had noticed. The generally putrid, stifling atmosphere had shielded the corpse's singular contribution. Nobody knew the man was dead except his partner, shackled in the berth with him, who'd said nothing because he'd been collecting the dead man's rations for himself.

'You arsehole,' the soldiers said. 'You stinking bloody bastard!'

Claudio de Pisera (a London felon with seven to serve) was shunned for the remainder of the journey, particularly by those fellow prisoners who knew in their hearts they would have done exactly the same.

THE WHITE MAN

With the Portuguese in charge, smuggling slaves into Cayenne had become difficult. If they caught the haul, every last Negro was confiscated and sent to Brazil to work the sugarcane. Dr Girodet's agent (originally from the Languedoc, called Dufrêne) had lost nearly fifty this way in only the last couple of months. He was getting fed up and was tired of the heavy forest trails he had to cut now to get across from Surinam, instead of sailing straight over from Paramaribo, easy as you like, the usual route he'd taken before.

'And if the fucking Portuguese don't take them, I lose half to fever on the way,' Dufrêne said. 'Or I've got to shoot a few because they refuse to get up and I've got to set an example for the rest of 'em. Or they run off because I can't afford extra hands to watch them. You know it's just me and the boy now.'

'The best you can do,' Dr Antoine Girodet said. 'It's all I ask, Dufrêne.'

'Ha! The best . . .'

Bergerard had come out of the main house and seen the lamps burning in the outbuilding windows. Dufrêne's come back, he thought, and stepped off the verandah. He'd hardly been gone a week and Bergerard was certain the man had returned empty-handed.

Dufrêne was with his son, Marcel, sitting at a table, a bottle of rum and glasses there, pistols, muskets and machetes in a loose pile, two pairs of bracelet manacles. They both had their boots off and legs stretched out before them, the stink of their raw, milky red feet hung in the fetid air.

'Here he is,' Dufrêne said. 'The timekeeper.' He was a wiry, angry, coiled man. His wife, it was said, had died from neglect.

By the far wall Bergerard saw a man sitting on the floor and leaning back, shackled wrists in his lap. Filthy and wearing torn clothes, covered in scratches, bites, bruises. Both eyes were swollen and his lips bloody. He smelled of sweat and the stink of alluvial mud, the piss-reek of river grass. A white man in chains.

'Where's the doctor?' Dufrêne asked.

'In the house,' Bergerard said. He was still looking at the man on the floor.

Dufrêne poured more rum into his glass. 'The rivers were flooded after the rains, we couldn't get through,' he said. 'Found this one on the way back. Almost fell over him.'

His son laughed. Marcel was short and plump, unlike his father in every way except liking his work.

'Who is he?' Bergerard said.

'Hasn't said a word since we picked him up,' Dufrêne said. Truth was, he'd beaten the man badly after the shock of seeing him suddenly there, leaning against a tree, as though he'd appeared up out of nowhere. 'But I'd say he's jumped a penal gang. They won't miss him. Thought he might be put to good use by you two.'

Bergerard turned towards the agent. He didn't like the man and it was all clear and plain in his face. Dufrêne saw it, held up his glass and grinned. Fucking Parisians, he thought. All he wanted was Girodet's money.

'To science!' he said and clinked his son's glass, threw back the rum. He poured another. 'To the furthering of human knowledge!'

There were footsteps outside. The door swung open and Girodet walked in.

'And look,' Dufrêne said, 'here comes the bloody devil himself!'

Dr Antoine Girodet stepped inside and immediately noticed the man sitting against the opposite wall. His first thought: *excellent.* A white man, someone to reason with. Mostly it was hell making the Negroes understand what he wanted of them; maybe this time it wouldn't be so frustrating.

'A gift for the wonderful doctor!' Dufrêne said.

'He's no good to me dead,' Girodet said. 'Have you given the man any water, food?'

'He's not dead yet,' Dufrêne said. 'And providing a man's last meal on earth isn't in our bargain, Monsieur Docteur de la guillotine.'

Girodet frowned, then looked at Bergerard. 'Tell the cook to bring something.' He pulled out a leather purse, tipped some coins into his hand and put the small stack on the table where the agent and his son were sitting.

'That's it?' Dufrêne said.

'Why? Have you something more for me?'

The agent swore. 'You can feed us at least, then.'

'I always do,' Girodet said. 'Christophe, and something for our friends here.'

Just then, the door to the outbuilding opened. Girodet turned to see Josephine over his shoulder. She was wearing clothes he'd given her (left behind by his wife), a yellow dress and white shawl. He knew why she'd come. He saw her scanning the room. Josephine had been asking about the slaves, the ones she'd been brought in with ('Where have they gone?') and all the others. Girodet told her the Portuguese had taken them.

'Why not me?' she'd said.

'Because you are mine.' He'd paid Dufrêne three times the money for her.

The agent now held up his glass. 'My beauty! My Josephine!'

She ignored Dufrêne and looked around, saw the white man sitting on the floor. He'd lifted his head up now and was squinting at her through his swollen eyes. And in that moment, Josephine saw her brother's *obia* hanging around the man's neck.

GREAT SOUTHERN LAND

They'd passed through the heads and into the great mouth of the harbour that was still like the wild sea, an enormous expanse of water fringed by rough-hewn sandstone cliffs and densely wooded hills of dry, dull green. A blustery wind threw sprays of foam and snapped the *Guildford*'s sails, leaned the mast; the timbers creaked and stretched, the ship reached up tall and carved the water with gleeful lunges of its bow. The sky was immense and swept clean, the palest, perfect blue.

Claus von Rolt shielded his eyes with the flat of his hand. Gulls swooped the hull, sleek and white, their harsh cries hungry.

The *Guildford* dropped anchor at ten o'clock in the morning. It was a Saturday. Passengers and most of the 73rd Regiment were disembarked first, while the convicts remained shackled below. Claus von Rolt could hear them underfoot as he crossed the deck, their chains dragging, the sound cold and woeful.

Sydney Cove was busy with construction: windmills and new stone docks, warehouses and trade buildings, barracks and roads. Rolt saw wagon carts loaded with quarried stone and surveyors at every corner, convicts labouring with picks and shovels, soldiers standing guard. Out past the clearings and towards the trees, small groups of blacks sat around smoky fires. The men were lean and tall, the women heavy-breasted, their laughing children running and playing in the sandy dirt.

He found lodgings on Bridge Street and spent his first night in the Antipodes listening to drunks outside his window. In the morning, he enquired about passage to the South Pacific and was told to ask at the docks, down where the whaling ships came in.

The captains were already in the taverns. They took a cup of rum when Rolt pulled out a coin and paid, but shook their heads at his request.

'It's the southern seas we ply, man, don't be daft. It's a working ship!'

They were coarse, bearded men, hands clawed, dry as brick, made stiff by hemp rope and harpoon, and with the fish stench of dead whale in their salty clothes. They looked at Rolt's fine tailoring and smiled.

'You'd get yourself all wet!'

They all said no.

An American whaler anchored in the late afternoon and Rolt went down to the dock again, still hopeful. The first man he saw come off the *New Bedford* wore a shrunken head around his neck. He was Māori. Rolt approached and spoke to him and the Māori pointed out his captain. Claus von Rolt offered double the money for passage.

'New Zealand's a way and the waters ain't pleasant,' the captain said.

'I've sea legs,' Rolt said, watching the barefoot Māori walk off with his crewmates.

'Well, good then. You'll need 'em. And I'll have the fare in advance.'

LETTERS

In Rio de Janeiro, Marta gave birth to a baby boy, brown and smooth and as shiny-dark-haired as she was.

'He will be Juan,' she said, but then she whispered another name into the child's ear, in Pataxó, which nobody would ever hear or know or be able to take from him, and this was the child's true secret name and it would protect him from possession and harm. It would remain between mother and son long after their bodies were corrupted and it would echo beyond them, through the infinite Great Forest, and for eternity.

The pregnancy had been easily hidden, as Marta didn't bloat in the way of white women, but with the birth now, of course, everything was different. It made things awkward for

Curado, who'd since returned from the wars in the Banda Oriental, alive and decorated. His wife would not have the Indian girl back to serve at their estancia anymore.

'She has disgraced herself and shamed God and her womanhood!' Curado's wife had said, and insisted Marta return the wooden crucifix that she'd once given her.

Without complaint, Marta took the necklace off and handed it to her master. The child was at her breast and she swept the soft hair from his sweaty forehead. She was relieved to be rid of the crucifix. Marta had always feared the symbol of the white Christ's terrible death. It was a yoke and now she was free of it.

'They'll both have to stay here,' Curado said, 'until you are released. And then . . .' The field marshal gestured with his hands, held them out. 'And then it will be as it will be.'

Général Fourés nodded, not really listening to what his friend was saying. He watched the little brown child being suckled. Ever since Marta had become pregnant, it had seemed to the général that he'd somehow slipped outside of his life and was watching it take place before him, as though it were somebody else's—or a dream.

'Juan,' he said, the child curled into his mother's breasts.

A whole new world had taken place in his prison cell. Where was France, where was Napoleon? Nowhere. They were nothing. And Juan was perfect, as beautiful as Marta, a brown cherub, an angel.

Earlier, Marta had painted a thick black stripe across Juan's tiny chest, and again over one half of his torso to the hips; then down his left arm with double lines (one roughly thicker than the other) and small connecting triangles between them, and two narrow bracelets around his plump wrists. The same motif was above and below his mouth, drawn out across his cheeks and to the ears on either side, all in dark black ink.

Curado had watched and been disturbed by Marta's tribal instincts. At the estancia, she'd been baptised and taught the Lord's Prayer and had always sat piously in the chapel while the priest swung the censer and splashed holy water with the aspergillum. But water couldn't penetrate skin. Could God even penetrate souls?

The boy was quiet. When Marta lifted him to the other breast, he cried, wriggled and kicked, desperate, then softened the instant her nipple was between his lips. Fourés couldn't account for the strength of his new love and desire for Marta.

'If you need anything, Michel . . .' Curado said (they called each other by their first names now). He smiled, almost sadly, paused at the door and then knocked for the guard to let him out.

In the weeks and months following, the général wrote Elisabeth many letters. He tried to capture in words all that had happened to him. He wrote and rewrote and read them over, but was unable to say one thing with certainty. Everything was true, but so much seemed to be missing, as though each word had only empty sky around it. The words wouldn't hold still, no matter how hard Fourés concentrated and firmly pledged them with the truth. His hammer slid from every nail head, struck none of them cleanly.

He tried to imagine Elisabeth before him, sitting in the chair, and wrote as he would have spoken to her, but all that fell to nonsense too.

Silence seemed to hold the only semblance of what his heart held: but what in God's name was a silent letter? He was a fool (of this he was certain).

Général Fourés tore up all the letters and threw them away.

Marta saw the strips of paper and wondered what they were. She knew only that her général frowned when he wrote them. It was best they were burned.

DREAMS OF CHINA

It was the Irish who said that China was nearby and it didn't matter that Johannes Meyer knew otherwise and said so.

'Been there before, right?' they said, and snarled at him, each man clinging desperate to the plan, for without China there was nothing but the impossible years lined up ahead and beyond.

'It's in the northern hemisphere,' Johannes said. 'This is the southern.'

'So it's just up the road a ways.'

Johannes had no idea of the wider geography of the world he'd been brought to, but considering how long it'd taken to sail here, he couldn't see a short walk to anywhere.

'You'll need water,' he said, 'food.'

'Yeah, well, the main thing is we won't be needin' *you.*'

(Laughter.)

They'd been sent north from Sydney Cove to Newcastle and mainly it was tree felling, upriver for a month inside huge stands of cedar, twelve-hour days and deadly snakes, the lash to coax their labour. Or it was the cliff mines for coal, shafts cut straight down into the sandstone, the sea spilling in and black lungs for the effort. But still, lime burning was the worst. Shells sliced their feet out on the mudflats where they fired the oyster beds and filled buckets of quicklime, the smoke burning their eyes raw and blind, a misery like no other.

The guards, to a man, were the cruellest under the Crown. There wasn't a convict soul didn't think about running, all the time, every day and every night.

'The blacks'll get you,' said the one they called Lacey, who'd himself absconded twice before but couldn't run again, his feet swollen and bruised blood crawling up his legs. 'They're cunning fucks!'

'I'll take me chances,' Dingle Donovan said, still scowling at Johannes Meyer. He was the leader here, among the ruined Irish bound for China. His teeth were as rotten as his soul, though they said he'd once been an upstanding man in

Kilkenny and could play the fiddle. 'The rest of you can stay and sew curtains with the German here.'

Two days later, twelve men and two women serving the officers' barracks absconded, soldiers in pursuit and blacks on their trail too, silent through the bush. Eight were returned inside a week, most of them found sitting down in the scrub or leaned back on a tree, waiting and in a daze, starving. The rest were left to their fates, predictable enough.

Dingle Donovan managed to stay out for two months. One day he limped back into the settlement, in rags and half-mad, his frail body broken out in sores and pustules from the hard sun, a spear wound festering in his leg, feet chewed and black. They tried to feed him but nothing stayed down. He died the next day on a cot in the hospital, no blanket spare to cover his corpse.

'What'd I say?' Lacey said and shook his head. 'Didn't I say it?'

THE ELECTRICAL MONK, BROTHER SALINAS

The abandoned hut was a low, rough thatching of branches and broad leaves, not far from the riverbank. Montoya ducked his head and looked in the doorway. He saw a sagging hammock and a stool on its side, a couple of wooden bowls on the ground and a box with its lid askew and bent on the hinges, a small pile of animal bones, some firewood, a rusted hatchet.

He turned to Elisabeth, who stood behind him. 'Well, he's not in there.'

She glanced into the hut. 'What now?'

Montoya took a deep breath, let it out slowly, thinking. He called over the two paddlers from the canoe, where they'd pulled up onto the riverbank. Each man shouldered a musket. Montoya pointed to a couple of openings in the forest near where they stood and sent each man to take a look.

'You think he's out for a walk?' Elisabeth said.

'Who knows?'

Elisabeth took off her hat and stepped into the shade of a tree. It was a scorching day. There'd been a slight breeze on the river, but here at the monk's hut there wasn't a whisper. She fanned herself with the brim of her hat and watched Montoya as he walked around the hut and looked over the ground. She'd resisted him and had nothing to regret, but felt ashamed now at her thoughts, which had succumbed and imagined much. Away from the settlement, alone with him here, she realised they would all come true.

'Maybe he went back to Caracas,' she said.

'Maybe.'

Elisabeth von Hoffmann could no longer endure a life of waiting. It had taken its toll and crept into her sleep. Waiting was no life and the général wasn't coming back and these were things she needed to attend to.

One of the paddlers came running out from the forest.

'Monsieur! Monsieur!' He'd found Brother Salinas.

Montoya told Elisabeth to wait but she ignored him. They followed the paddler back through the forest, twisting through the thick and tangled growth.

'The monk,' the paddler said, 'he lives in a tree!'

The tree was enormous, the size of a cathedral. They couldn't see him at first, but then Brother Salinas threw something (narrowly missing Montoya) and the paddler took the musket from his shoulder and pointed up into the foliage.

'There he is!'

They saw him. He was standing on a huge branch, one hand holding onto the branch above, dressed in rags that must have once been a cassock, his long legs bare, his head completely bald and white against the green all around him. He stared down at them and said nothing.

'Brother Salinas!' Montoya called out, moving closer. 'I have come a long way to see you!'

The monk picked up something on the branch beside him, cocked his free arm and threw whatever it was at Montoya; again, it almost struck him. The paddler put the musket to his shoulder.

'Be calm,' Montoya said. 'Put the barrel down.'

'He is crazy!'

Montoya turned to Elisabeth. 'Stay where you are.'

She smiled at the serious look on his face. 'The hairless man of genius,' she said. 'In a tree.'

'Brother Salinas! My name is Alejandro Joaquin Montoya! I have come to speak with you of science!'

Monkeys screeched higher up in the tree, their faces peering through the leaves to see what was happening. Then the monk suddenly called out, a wild, high-pitched imitation of the sound, and Montoya took an involuntary step back.

'By God!'

Another projectile came flying through the air.

'Ask him about the ice machine,' Elisabeth said.

'What are you doing, man?' Montoya said, angry now. 'Desist!'

The monk threw something again and shrieked like a monkey. The other monkeys above joined him in an excited, piercing chorus.

The paddler crouched down beside one of the projectiles on the ground, looked it over and then grimaced in disgust. It was a hardened piece of excrement. Human. The monk's own.

'He's shitting on us!'

Back in the canoe, Montoya cursed the man vehemently, until Elisabeth's laughter was too much for him to resist.

'That's the last time I take you anywhere,' he said.

OBIA

When Krüger opened his eyes it was night, but the windows were silvered with moonlight. She was standing above him, a ring of keys in her hand, a soft glowing lamp in the other. It was true, what Mr Hendrik had said; she was the most beautiful girl he'd ever seen.

'Tell me,' Josephine said.

His mouth was dry, he could barely swallow. 'Water.'

She put the keys and the lamp down, fetched him a cup.

'Tell me,' she said.

Krüger held up the empty cup. The shackles clinked, fluid, hard, water and stone together. 'More,' he said.

She went and poured him another. He listened intently to the sound of her bare feet padding over the floorboards.

'Tell me,' she said.

He drank the tepid water but was no nearer to quenching his thirst. He put the empty cup beside him.

'You kill Mr Hendrik.'

'No.'

'You see him killed.'

'No.'

Josephine kneeled down, sat on her heels.

'He wanted me to take you away,' Krüger said.

'Dead don't want nothin'.'

'We should go from this place.'

Josephine looked away. 'He was my brother.'

'The keys.'

She pointed at his chest, at the *obia* there. 'Don't you know?' she said, appalled at his ignorance.

The weight on Krüger's body was sudden. He gasped, coughed. The pain in his ribs was sharp.

'You know it,' she said. 'Accept.'

Krüger grimaced, but took strength from her shining eyes. She looked away, disappointed.

'No changing it,' she said.

'We can go, together we can go. I will take you.'

Josephine shook her head. From somewhere in the front of her dress, she took out a pipe. She tamped tobacco into the bowl, took a long, thin splinter of wood and lifted the glass on the lamp, lit the splinter off the lazy oil flame. She brought it to the tobacco in the pipe and puffed.

'Mr Hendrik suffer,' she said.

'He loved you.'

Josephine closed her eyes, rocked back and forth a little. 'And he suffer.'

'The keys.' Krüger held up his shackled wrists.

She frowned. 'Where you go?'

'Together we go.'

'No buyin' nothin' no money.'

'The keys.' He dropped his hands into his lap.

'Listen,' Josephine said. She pointed at the *obia* again with her pipe. 'You hear it.'

Krüger closed his eyes, the lids heavy as chains.

'Listen tell it.'

'No!'

Josephine reached over and put her hand to Krüger's forehead. Her hand was soft and cool.

'Listen tell it, man.'

He breathed in the smell of her palm. The touch of her skin, her fingertips. Tears pooled in his eyes. She whispered something in a language he couldn't understand.

'Don't go,' he said. 'Don't leave me.'

'No,' she said, but reluctantly. Then she stayed like that beside him and smoked her pipe until he fell asleep.

NGĀTI KURI

Blown violently off course by a storm in the Tasman Sea, the *New Bedford* was driven south of the Manawatawhi islands, ripped and raked across the living ocean. Fury surged tremendous flanks of dark water and crashing waves and men were washed away from the deck like tiny crabs. She struck the reef just after midnight: five hundred and seventy-nine barrels of whale oil to the bottom, twenty-nine men, the captain and his log, every hull rivet, ship timber and mast, the sails long lost to the gales that had torn and snapped them away to the horizon.

Seven survivors, including Claus von Rolt, washed ashore onto a rocky, coarse-sanded beach.

Over the stormed hours of that night, they dragged themselves out of the heavy water one by one, brine lung'd, salt-bleached, the bitter burn of the sea in the backs of their throats. Prostrate, grateful, pummelled, penitent, they fisted the cold sand and thanked Almighty God.

All except Rolt, who thanked only the warrior's shrunken head, still hanging by the cord around his neck.

They waited for dawn, shivering. In the morning, the beach was strewn with broken timbers and debris from the smashed ship. Bodies of the drowned began to wash up too, waxen and blue, draped in sashes of green-black kelp. The Ngāti Kuri tribesmen came as they were struggling to bury the dead in the hard-packed, shell-crusted ground.

The Ngāti Kuri wielded their *patu paraoa* and clubbed each man to death, the first blow knocking the half-drowned men senseless, the second and third to oblivion. Claus von Rolt was last, his tattooed killer pausing to laugh at the head Rolt wore around his neck. The man reached out and snapped the cord off with one pull, held the shrunken head up to his companions, who each turned and either laughed or smiled, or were deeply offended by what they saw and spoke angrily.

Had this white man come to conquer them with such pathetic powers and such disrespect?

The Ngāti Kuri warrior threw the shrunken head away. Claus von Rolt lunged for it, but was knocked backwards and onto the ground with a blow from the man's heavy club. Then he thrust at Rolt with his *pouwhenua*, stabbing him under the ribcage. The smooth, broad wooden blade slid easily into the Prussian's flesh, piercing his lung and hitting the spine. The warrior leaned on it, heard a rib crack, then pulled the weapon clear. He reached up high and it was the last thing Claus von Rolt ever saw, the man's tattooed face and the wild cry he made, eyes shining, the terrible, gaping, red flesh hole of his open mouth.

GOOD CONDUCT

There were plenty of opportunities to escape (the camp was loose, the guards corrupt) and it was all Johannes Meyer could think about, but he resisted the urge to run. Along with the evidence of his fellow convicts and their failed attempts, he sensed a misalignment of time and place. There was an instinct to wait, and he abided.

He suffered, survived the miserable days, though they defeated him often enough. Nothing he'd ever experienced compared to what he now endured.

He held on.

'They nabbed Larson,' somebody said in the dark, each man chained to his pallet.

'Bates?'

'Dead.'

'Good riddance.'

'Fuck you!'

'Just try it, brother!'

Johannes Meyer held on. Something in his ear told him to.

26 MARCH 1812

Alejandro Joaquin Montoya and Elisabeth von Hoffmann boarded a ship in Cayenne and sailed for Caracas, in Venezuela.

There, after converting to Catholicism (a single morning's administering of the rites of Holy Communion and Confirmation, followed by a generous donation to the priest), Elisabeth and Montoya were married in the Iglesia de San Francisco, on a steamy Wednesday afternoon. Apart from the priest and two altar boys, and an old woman in black who kneeled and prayed silently by a glowing stand of candles (she'd walked in as the ceremony began, a dark figure in a harsh blaze of light in the doorway), there was in attendance only a lawyer acquaintance of Montoya's, who served as witness and later toasted them in his home.

'To a long and happy life with many sons and daughters!'

They stayed in Caracas for three weeks and enjoyed each other with passion and abandon, reaping every day the satisfactions of new and deeper intimacies.

For the first time since leaving Berlin, Elisabeth Montoya wrote her aunt Margaretha a letter. She told her aunt of her marriage and happiness. She wrote one to Général Fourés too, care of the authorities in Cayenne and in the hope that he might receive it one day. She wrote of how much she missed him and of the loss of their love and her shame that she could not hold him close again, that time had withered her strength. *Another man has come to love me*, she wrote, a gift, as he had once been. She hoped, and she knew, he would not think ill of her.

Elisabeth went early to send the letters and returned to their room in a state of bliss, these last duties to her former life performed, her guilt unburdened in some way, enough at least for now.

On this particular day, that was also the eve of their departure for Montoya's home in Valdivia, it was unusually hot. Not a breath of wind, only a disconcerting stillness. The residents of Caracas were all in the streets and gathering for Holy Thursday, and they went early to find a seat in the coolness of the churches. The strange quiet (there wasn't a single bird in the sky or in the trees or perched on the eaves of houses) and the deadness of the air was seen to reflect the solemnity of the day and the power of God's will.

Montoya looked out from the balcony of their room and watched the procession of people. He wanted to go for a walk through the streets, but Elisabeth wouldn't get up again and stayed in bed. She watched him dress and pull his boots on.

'Bring back something to eat,' she said as Montoya bent down to kiss her. 'It's too hot to go anywhere.'

'Señora Montoya,' he said, 'I never dreamed you would be so lazy.'

Elisabeth dozed beneath the bedsheet, her legs out to the sides, exhausted by the heat and by love, deeply contented. Some time later she woke when a bead of sweat trickled down the back of her knee. She wiped at it with her other leg and turned over in the bed, luxuriating in her happiness and the warm scent of her new husband on the pillows. She wondered when Montoya would return, relishing his absence as she imagined him coming back through the door. She finally got out of bed and had water brought to the room so that she could take a bath. Afterwards, Elisabeth sat in a rocking chair and drank coffee and smoked one of Montoya's thin cigars.

It was now seven minutes past four.

First, everything shook and there was a deep rumbling sound like thunder and the church bells began to ring erratically. The bath spilled its water and the furniture walked the room. Vases, lamps, pictures were upended and smashed into pieces on the floor.

Then a pause, a moment: not a sound, only the tinkling of glass, the chandelier above Elisabeth's head. There was a sensation of everything being sucked into a hole, of everything rushing silently down, through the floor, down into a drain.

She went to the window, moving as though through some kind of thickness, the air condensed into matter. And then there was another cracking, dry, terrific booming sound and the building started to shake violently again. Elisabeth saw a wave pass through everything outside, as though the city had become liquid. She saw the ground tear open and split apart and the buildings of Caracas toppled over and collapsed, fell into gaping crevices. Great clouds of dust burst into the air; it was hard to see any distance. There was yelling and screaming in the streets.

And in that instant, the balcony fell from Elisabeth's room, and then the entire facade of the building dropped away. She saw people falling through the air, women, children, dogs and cats. The bath tipped completely now and the water rushed out across the floor, swept over Elisabeth's bare feet and ankles. She looked down and the shock that had taken hold of her broke. She ran for the door and onto the landing and began down the twisted, splintered staircase, no mind to anything but getting out, getting out.

WOURALI DREAMS

Girodet was frustrated and grew angry. He struck Krüger across the face with the back of his hand, split the skin over the cheekbone, which instantly began to bleed, cut by the ring on Girodet's finger.

And still the man remained delirious and unreachable.

'He won't agree,' Girodet said.

'He doesn't understand,' Christophe Bergerard said. 'He's in a fever.'

'Damnation!'

'There's nothing to be done.'

Girodet stood up. 'He'll still add numbers to our ledger,' he said. 'If not insight to our cause.'

Bergerard nodded, looking down at the man, who was at their mercy. 'Hopefully he'll stay alive long enough,' he said.

Josephine watched through the window. She waited until the doctor and Bergerard were gone, then came in and kneeled down beside Krüger.

She pressed some of the gummy wourali paste she'd made into the cut across his cheek. It only ever worked if it entered the bloodstream.

'Sleep,' she said. 'Dream.'

Snakes' teeth (labarri, counacouchi), vines, dried roots, ants, Indian peppers. She'd learned the recipe from her brother, Mr Hendrik, who'd learned it from the forest Indians in Surinam.

'There be no more living to suffer, man,' Josephine said, smearing the paste. 'Let bad heart go.'

Shave the vine and roots, pour water on the shavings, drain into a calabash. Smash the vines stalks and crush the root flesh, squeeze the juice out. Bruise the snake fangs and mash the ants. Throw them in, all together, everything mixed and then into a clay pot. Cook over a low fire, slow, slow, ladle away the scum, cook and cook until thick and dark, dark brown, like burnt sugar.

Whisper the name of thy enemy or friend, whisper and sing their dreams.

'It is not a woman's work,' Mr Hendrik said, when she'd first asked him for the secret. 'Not for you.'

She begged and pestered, knew he wouldn't deny her.

'It will call the evil down and curse you!' he said.

'He is here already!' she said. 'Look, brother, look! It is the captain!'

'No!'

But he showed Josephine how to make it, what to do.

'Do not eat for a day and the morning before, then not for another day and the morning after. The pot must be new, never used, and never after, and always the red clay pot. Do not breathe its boiling breath.' He gathered the ingredients, spoke over them, bashed them with the handle of a machete, and showed her the order and the time everything took. 'Be exact,' he said. 'You will be sick for three days after. Do not fear. Leave and be alone, do not speak to women, and never the young women and never none weighed with child. The breath will be in you for these three days but then it will leave and you will recover.'

It had taken her some days to gather all that was necessary. And yes, she had been sick. She painted more wourali paste across Krüger's cut cheek.

'Better this way,' she said. 'You dream all there to see. And my brother too, Mr Hendrik be free. He dream some place, you see it.'

Outside, rain began to pummel the ground. It fell in a great roar and within seconds everything was mud and spreading pools of water.

Josephine took red and yellow parrot feathers out from her sleeve, wove them into the *obia* around Krüger's neck. It was to aid the spirit flying and to give strength. There were enough feathers for Mr Hendrik, too (they were joined by the *obia* and must fly together). They were brothers in death.

Krüger's limbs became heavy, and then he couldn't feel them anymore, only vaguely, and then he forgot about them. His neck stiffened and his heart slowed, slowed, he heard it as though from far away. And then the heartbeat was a voice, calling him, come, and then it was singing, singing.

Josephine stayed beside the white man, sang softly and listened to the rain as it washed the world clean.

BOOK VIII

BOOK VIII

THE PENULTIMATE DEFEAT; OR,
A MOMENTARY DIVERSION

He tried to kill himself but survived the vial of poison (it was only a half-attempt, really, the valet said in private). When he woke the next morning (exhausted, thirsty, pale), the world was still as he had left it. The Russians had occupied Paris and he'd been exiled to the island of Elba in the Mediterranean. It appeared the gods wished him to endure a little longer.

But the climate down there, the Italians, the clear blue sea, it was something like Corsica. When he stepped off the ship in Portoferraio, a huge crowd of people had gathered to greet him.

'*Viva l'imperatore!*'

Bonaparte quickly revived. His boots were polished for hours, his stride lengthened. With a personal army of some twelve hundred soldiers, two or three small ships (he referred to them as his navy) and an entourage of workers, footmen, valets, chefs and secretaries bequeathed to him by the victors, he set about improving what he saw as the miserable lot of Elba's inhabitants.

He planted trees, cleaned the streets and organised garbage collectors. He improved the water supply and established gardens, irrigated new crops. They said there hadn't been a man possessed of such boundless energy since—well, they couldn't remember when. There had never been such a man before!

Only the news of Josephine's death could halt his constant, relentless advance. When Bonaparte was told of it, he stayed in his rooms for three days and refused to see anybody.

Further days passed, weeks, months; the Emperor endured. He wrote to his wife, the Empress Marie-Louise (every morning, every day), but the Empress stalled and made excuses, until finally she resented his demands for her presence on Elba. ('It is only his reputation he cares about,' she was told, repeatedly, by her entourage of minders. 'You must forget him.') Soon enough, she did forget him and succumbed to the many charms of her handsome chaperone, General Graf von Neipperg. Then she never opened another letter from Bonaparte again.

He tried to keep busy, but his false enthusiasms were exposed and shivered into dust, every day by day. For truly, there was nothing to match his ambition there on Elba. Where was he? Nowhere! The scale, it was all wrong, reduced. The world was out of proportion.

An island wasn't nearly enough.

He endured. Then finally, after three hundred days on the island of Elba, Napoleon Bonaparte escaped.

LUCKY BREAK

They gave him a conditional pardon (half free, that is, until further notice) and changed his name at the same time. John Myer in the paperwork now, everything official, Lieutenant Governor Lachlan Macquarie signed it and there was nothing else for Johannes to think about.

Until they caught him two months later receiving stolen ewes. Judge George Tobias Fitzgerald presiding, in his yellowing wig and with his various ailments, sentenced John Myer again, another fourteen years' hard labour down in Van Diemen's Land.

He didn't say a word (of course, he wasn't permitted to say a word) and he looked up at the judge and had an out-of-body experience: Johannes Meyer was actually in Berlin, dreaming that this was happening to him, or to somebody who might have been him. Somebody they called John Myer. He didn't know who this man was and, suddenly, it was a relief! It made him feel calm, because he knew that soon he'd be waking up from all this. He'd be able to go for a walk down Unter den Linden, and later visit Otto's on Taubenstraße and drink good coffee, listen to the philosophers argue. What had become of the one called Krüger?

John Myer knew the sheep were stolen. All the sheep, everywhere, were stolen. Everything in the colony was stolen.

'Wha'd'you want with bloody sheep?' she said.

He should have listened to Kathleen. She'd wanted to lease the small house in York Street, rent out the back room to lodgers and sell them a bite, a bottle of beer, her exclusive night-time comforts (mostly it was that). 'I need a man about,' she'd said, loud into his ear because the grog shop was raucous, the Rocks at its debauched heights. 'Someone I can trust,' she said, 'no bloody drunk, no basher.' She leaned back a little, smiled kindly, smoothed John Myer's hair across his forehead and came back to his ear. 'Someone pretty like you, eh?' And with a few coins in your pocket and the right signatures in your book, she thought. Because they wouldn't lease shit to the likes of her.

Eighteen, and her breath rusty with rum. They'd met at the Ferret's place, a dingy hole, and John Myer couldn't even remember the first time, he'd drunk so much, fresh in his freedom; stumbling through the night, a thin mattress on a dirt floor somewhere, waking with his head cleaved. 'There's money owed,' she'd said in the cold morning, standing above him. 'You can buy us breakfast.'

That morning, in the streets, the mist like cannon smoke, drifting, whispering death. Kathleen's blue face. And the girl again, in the window, who'd looked at him, who looked at him now. John Myer called out, still drunk, but what would that do? It wouldn't do a thing.

Damper loaf and dark ale, she ate more than half, drank most of the bottle. His only friend in the colony then. Kathleen of the kind brown eyes and hair the colour of stale biscuit, who wore the same tattered maroon dress most nights, patched and sewn.

'Wha'd'you say, pretty John? Do we have a deal?'

He bought the ewes instead (he didn't even know they were ewes). There was plenty of cheap land outside of town. John Myer was searching for peace, though it was true he mainly went about drinking for it.

'What would you rather?' he said, hoping she'd agree to come with him.

Kathleen laughed. She'd have no more of that work, she said. The stink of wet wool and pellets of shit slimy in the rain, the dreary long days of her girlhood.

She washed back into the crowd, down at the Rocks, gone.

The soldiers came for him, on the very morning he got his sheep, a set-up plain from the start. Seven sheep there, plump too, but the soldier boys only counted four in the ledger.

UPON HIS RELEASE, THE GÉNÉRAL HAPPILY RETIRES FROM THE LIFE HE ONCE KNEW

Field Marshal Curado said, 'Where will you go?'

Marta, heavily pregnant again, wore Juan strapped to her back and she rolled clothes into bundles, gathered their things from around the room. Curado and the général stood watching her, cups of dark rum in their hands.

'Somewhere quiet,' Fourés said.

'You will not return to Cayenne? Or to France?'

'It would be no life for Marta and the children in either place,' Fourés said, looking at his young family. 'Nor for me.'

Curado had expected it. He slipped out some folded documents from his pocket. 'These will help you pass through the territories,' he said, handing them over. 'Beyond that is beyond my control and forecast.'

The général thanked him.

'I cannot dissuade you?' the field marshal said. 'The wild lands are volatile, things change by the day.'

Fourés touched Curado on the arm and smiled. 'That is the whole world, my friend,' he said. 'There's no escaping it.'

Curado glanced at Marta. 'They're different, you know. From you and I.'

'Yes,' Fourés said. It was beyond him to explain in words. Marta wanted nothing of him, she'd placed no obligations on his shoulders, and yet there he was, heart brimming for her, the bond between them unbreakable.

'I wish you good fortune, Général.'

A final look around the room. Marta checked under the bed.

'Away now,' Fourés said.

The guard brought their things down to the street. Curado had supplied Fourés with a small horse, a musket, pistol and ammunition, a dagger and an axe, some supplies. From his own pommel, he retrieved the général's cavalry sabre, from so long ago, cleaned and polished and the scabbard shining black and silver.

'Sharpened and without a speck of rust,' Curado said.

'I am in your debt.'

'It has been my privilege.'

Fourés wrapped the belt around the scabbard and sword, tucked it into one of their bags. Everything was tied securely to the horse.

The two men kissed, holding shoulders, then braced at arm's length.

'Goodbye.'

Curado handed Marta the wooden crucifix he'd taken from her before (she took it silently and let it dangle from her hand). Then he watched them walk away, down the hill past the monastery: the Frenchman, his Indian woman and their child, like a small family of peasants, all they owned hanging from the horse's pommel.

TWO PER MUSKET IS THE STANDARD RATE

Claus von Rolt's head was tattooed and then cut off high on the neck. His brain was removed and the cavity filled with flax and gum, the nostrils too, then his eyes were scooped out and the sockets plugged with the same fibrous paste, and the lids were sewn shut. His tongue was thrown to a dog. A fire was lit and stones were heated in it; Rolt's head was buried with the hot stones until the moisture had been steamed out. Afterwards, his head was recovered and smoked over another fire, then hung and left to dry out completely in the sun and wind.

The Ngāti Kuri had Rolt and the six other heads they'd collected that morning on the shipwrecked beach, plus the heads of four more bodies the sea had washed up. Tattooed, smoked and preserved, their skin turned dark brown and blackened, their hair matted and darkened coal black too, noses stretched, ears shrivelled, and ragged, bone-white teeth protruded from between thinned, retracted lips that were curled gruesomely. It was impossible to tell they weren't Māori, or that the tattooed markings were a fabrication and meaningless.

Through an interpreter, the chief of the Ngāti Kuri told the Englishman James Crowell the story of their recent battle with a rival tribe, of the fearsome warriors they had bravely faced and slain, of the blood that had been spilled. He indicated where the imaginary battle had taken place. (Crowell turned and looked to where the chief pointed, seeing all that was described to him and laying it down in his memory. He would embellish and retell the story later to his eager collectors.) When the chief finished his story, he pointed to the eleven *toi moko* that had been stuck to wooden stakes driven into the ground. He said, 'Eleven muskets.'

The Englishman James Crowell listened to the interpreter. He shook his head and held up two fingers.

'Two heads,' Crowell said, nodding towards the *toi moko*. Now he held up a forefinger. 'One musket.' He put an imaginary rifle to his shoulder. 'Tell the chief it's the standard rate.'

The chief of the Ngāti Kuri frowned. His warriors stared intently at the Englishman. A few walked around and came to stand nearer, tall and muscled and fearsome. Every hair on James Crowell's body tightened at the root.

The chief spoke again and crossed his arms.

The interpreter turned to the Englishman, began to speak, but Crowell interrupted him. 'Yes, yes, I understand,' he said. The tribes were upping the price; they had come to realise the value of the preserved heads and sought better remuneration. Their tribal wars had become intense, all over the island, and the trade in smuggled rifles had proliferated. There'd been lots of rumours, of missing and murdered traders who'd attempted to swindle them. And there was no doubting the aggressive, distrustful mood here. Behind James Crowell, the nervousness of his men was palpable.

'Sir,' one of them said, 'just give 'em the bloody rifles and let's get back to the ship.'

Crowell adjusted the figures in his mind; there was still money to be made. Not as much, but profit nonetheless. And better he was around to spend it.

He smiled at the Māori chief and indicated the musket crates stacked on the ground near his men.

'Ask the great chief if he requires any instruction in their use.'

'It will not be necessary,' the interpreter said.

The heads were wrapped in oilskins and canvas, stowed on the ship in a waterproof trunk. Later that year, Claus von Rolt passed through Customs House in Sydney. *Baked head* was recorded in the inventory ledger.

HOBART TOWN GAOL IS FULL OF HOLES

Into the cell, over the troubled dream-breathing of the shackled men, came the sound of breaking waves. Punchy but small, a rushed gravel splash. River waves, not really waves at all.

Lying on the wooden pallet, John Myer turned his head to listen. They seemed at once close and then suddenly distant. But in the night dark, in the agitated silence, they were enough.

He closed his eyes and remembered the beach in San Sebastián, where he'd slept on the coarse yellow sand. He lay on the pallet and longed for the roar of those Basque sea waves, the long rolling crush. His toes in the cold sand, the moon, the stars, the vastness in every direction, starving but free. Salt and sea mist, cool over his arms and face.

Better not to think it. He knew you only ever came back to where you were. But the taste remained sweet on his lips.

The guard's boots now, down the corridor, the slow clip, the oiled clack of a musket over his shoulder.

John Myer dropped his reverie.

There was the sound of keys, the dry clatter of the lock. The shuddering creak of hinges, the heavy door swung open.

A whisper. 'Turner?'

'Aye,' the whisper back.

'Now.'

The one called Turner said, 'Let's go, boys.'

Chains clinked as they stood up, different heights, silhouettes of rags in the dark. They'd all chipped in on the bribe: a silver ring, a brooch, a chain, dented rum flasks and tobacco tins and pipes, whatever they'd been able to gamble or smuggle up their arses. Anything shiny a magpie might filch. A king's ransom in trinkets.

The guard said, 'Not a fucking word.' It was a nice little earner, working the gaol, every now and then.

AFTERMATH

Twenty thousand people perished in the earthquake that levelled Caracas. Among them was Elisabeth Montoya's husband, Alejandro Joaquin Montoya. The only person in the entire decimated city who Elisabeth knew (and who'd also survived as she had) was the lawyer who'd witnessed and then celebrated their wedding.

Rodrigo Felipe Francisco Ojeda eventually found Elisabeth and couldn't believe it. He stood before her amid the ruins, his eyes raw and dark-circled. Then he smiled with warmth and sad resignation.

'You're alive,' he said. He embraced her. She felt very thin in his arms and he let go quickly. Ojeda had come to look for the newlyweds, through the rubble and devastation, the crushed bodies, through the city shaken apart and crumbled, and the crying children, tears streaking their dry chalked cheeks.

He'd brought a small parcel of food and some brandy.

'I have lost everything,' he said. His wife, a daughter and son-in-law, his mother, his house, his neighbours. Ojeda hadn't slept for days. He needed to bring horses and wagons down from his country estancia to help in the recovery of bodies, to deliver supplies. He had to do something, if only not to think, not to be overwhelmed and paralysed, his own life ended.

'I am sorry for your loss, Elisabeth Montoya,' he said. 'For all our losses.' He wiped his brow with a handkerchief. 'He was my friend.'

They stood in silence, the heavy silence of fallen mountains. Then Ojeda said, 'You must come with me. There is no place else for you to go.'

Together they left the canvas shelter that had been erected for survivors and where Elisabeth had been staying, bewildered and unable to comprehend or believe what had happened.

They walked through endless ruins and misery and horror. A boy with a donkey and cart took them some of the way. He whistled, as though nothing had happened.

At his estancia in the mountains, the lawyer signed fresh affidavits confirming the legality of Elisabeth's marriage to Montoya (the original documents had been lost in the catastrophe). After she'd rested and recovered and some of the shock had loosened its grip on her, the lawyer convinced Elisabeth that she must travel to Valdivia and claim her husband's property.

'You could stay here, I would not object; I would happily share all that I have. But then you would live forever in this grief, this memory,' the lawyer said. 'There is nothing for you here. You are a young woman. It is only right that you should receive what he has left behind and I know that Alejandro would have wished it so.'

He gave her some money and a few of his wife's dresses and her rosary beads. Elisabeth would never forget his kindness and generosity, but she was afraid and reluctant to leave. She was alone again. And for the first time since she'd left Berlin with the général, Elisabeth was tempted by the idea of return. Just go home, she thought. But in the moment of thinking it, she knew: there was no truth to the idea and there never had been.

AGAIN, THE MARCH; AGAIN, THE CALL OF DRUMS

The story is well known (six hundred loyal men, cheering crowds along the way, King Louis XVIII fleeing the Tuileries) but not everybody watched with love, or even vague interest, as Napoleon Bonaparte triumphantly returned to Paris. Talleyrand had sighed at the news, perfectly aware of what to expect

('Farce,' he said to the Duc d'Otrante, 'affectation, ranting.'), while the gods had yawned and glanced down from on high, taking the scene in only briefly, distractedly. They saw straight off that it was the same man on the same white horse, with the same simple desires, and rubbed their sleepy eyes.

'He's still here?'

With the pure intent of his will, yes, he was still here, but what was human will to the gods? They stretched leisurely, turned over. 'Wake us in Waterloo,' they said.

Josephine's daughter Hortense met with Bonaparte in Paris, as did the Countess Walewska and one or two former lovers, all wondering if the gleam would still be there in his eyes. They supposed it was, but of course so much had happened, the effect on them was different. The old energy seemed renewed, but the flesh was pale, the hair thinner, strands stuck to his sweating forehead.

'I'm off to Malmaison,' he said to Hortense. 'Will you accompany me?'

They arrived in the late afternoon. He sat in her mother's room alone, the door closed, a hushed silence throughout the house, servants afraid of making a sound. Hortense wished she hadn't come.

Back in Paris, Bonaparte wrote to the Empress, but no, never. Marie-Louise would never come now.

Waterloo came and then went. They tried to wake them but the gods slept through the whole thing.

FREEDOM

There were six of them waiting in the barn. The old man who came was burly and short, a thick-forearmed man, serious and intent on his task. He said, 'There,' and pointed to where a lamp glowed on the ground. He didn't want to know their names and kept his own to himself, and all he did was point to the spot on the chopping block where he wanted them to drape their chains.

He held the heavy chisel over the locked clasps, carefully adjusting the blunt tip with his knotted fingers, then suddenly wielded the hammer (an ugly, rusty cube of iron that seemed to grow out of his fist), swung it with such speed and concentrated power that each man flinched and the horse whinnied and stamped in his stall. He struck powerfully with three successive *plink plink plinks* (all it took) and the locks burst open under blows that would have crushed all the bones in their feet or severed their hands from their wrists, if not for the iron around them and the man's precision.

'Jesus!'

John Myer had his turn and was released. He felt the exhilaration of the shackles cracking like eggs and sliding to the ground, the instant lightness in his arms and legs. Now he was a man again and it was almost as though he were light enough to fly.

Turner was the last who needed unshackling and balanced a foot on the block. Ankles first, then down on his knees for the wrists. He was blue-eyed and sunken-cheeked, scrawly tattoos down his back and arms. They said he'd tried to sail a jolly boat up the New South Wales coast, except the waves tipped him out and then the sun scorched him dry. And then they sent him down here, but he was having none of it.

'Bless me, Father,' he said, 'for I have sinned.'

'Thou art wicked and unworthy.'

'Aim straight, you old bastard.'

'Best you hold still then, pumpkin.'

Their tone was warm: they knew each other. And there was a young girl there too, who stood among them all, holding another lamp and a shawl tight at her chest. She smiled and Turner gave her a wink. The old man busted the last shackles, a few drops of sweat at his temples now. Turner stood up and flexed his wrists, then took a jacket the young girl brought over to him, punched his fists into the sleeves.

'When's the master and his family back?' Turner said.

'In the morning,' the girl said.

Turner looked at the old man. 'Drop the hammer and chisel there, leave the chains as they've fallen.'

'I'm not stupid, laddie.' The old man's fingerprints were baked into the bricks that were the Hobart Town Gaol. He was no stranger to shackles or running.

Turner grinned. 'Rum?'

'I've bread and some bacon,' the girl said.

'And there's rum,' her father said.

One of the convict boys said, 'We're goin' t'eat now?'

'You can do whatever the hell you like, Robbie,' Turner said.

The boy looked down at the pile of chains, pale and nervous.

They sat down around the lamp on the hay-strewn ground, shared the bacon and bread and rum. When they'd finished, the old man held out a coil of rope to Turner.

'The sun'll be here soon,' he said.

Turner nodded and stood up. The old man gave the convict his back, crossed hands at the wrists. 'Nice and tight now,' he said.

'Mister?' The girl was sitting beside John Myer. She held out more rope and turned her back to him and John Myer tied up her wrists. The girl's arms were thin and white, her hands small, the lines in her palms silted. She watched Turner, silently, as John Myer tied her wrists. And he thought, all this way, all these years, to tie this young girl's hands.

Turner saddled the horse. He kissed the young girl on the head and whispered in her ear. She looked with longing and tearful eyes as he took the reins.

'Ainsley's farm,' he said to the rest of them. 'Two days from now.' And then he smacked the old man on the shoulder and walked the animal out of the barn. They heard the thudding of the horse's hoofs fade away.

John Myer glanced at the old man and then at the girl, both on the ground and leaning back against a railing. Only she was looking up at him.

'Quick about it, then,' the old man said. 'Out with you.'

The morning light had already begun to spread. Soon a heavenly orange hazed the sky above the hills beyond the river, smudged the lower cloud bellies pink. It was John Myer's first glimpse of this Van Diemen's Land. He'd come in the night and then fled in it, too. At last the light. The sky reminded him of somewhere he'd been before.

The river was flat, without a ripple, sheens of glass-blue and silver. They were somewhere north of Hobart Town. A few houses spaced across the hills and clearings, dark stands of trees between.

'We have to go north-west,' the boy Robbie said, pointing into the thickly forested distance of more hills, fold into fold.

Half an hour later they'd just made the tree line when the fog swept over them. They stopped, stunned and curious. Looking up, the sky was gone, the earth devoured. They could barely see each other. John Myer could only make out the sun, low and veiled and whetstoned into a pure white disc.

'What should we do?' the boy asked.

'Wait, you fool.'

The fog swept fast down the river valley, shrouding the world in white shadowness.

They waited; it was pointless to continue. They waited, until they heard the crunch of boots through the scrub.

A few took off, but everybody was caught.

HE GOES BAREFOOT LIKE AN INDIAN
AND EATS WITH HIS HANDS

There was talk that he'd been a general in Napoleon's Grande Armée, but when they saw him in the flesh, well, it was diffi-cult to believe.

He was known as Miguel now (no longer Michel) and he owned a cocoa plantation near Itacaré, south of the Rio de Contas. Trade had been lucrative, the years favourable, his hand in the business as natural as it once had been upon his sword. Upset on occasion by weather or war, sometimes both, but such was life. He drank it all down, deep. Often, as he lay in a hammock and stared up into the flickering leaves, the bright sky beyond, he'd try to trace the course of his life, pairing off sequences and events that had led to this moment, to this hammock, this glimpse of endless tropical sky. If not for the Portuguese, no arrest; if not for his arrest, no Curado; if not for Curado, no Marta et cetera. He'd reach back through his mind, hold the course, and yet was unsure as to what exactly he was searching for. Some action authored by his will, not another's? Possibly (yes, that was it). Hours in the hammock, he only ever arrived at Bonaparte.

Miguel, when he could, went swimming. He'd learned how at the age of fifty-two and discovered a great love of the water, the breaking surf. He also drew and painted, pictures of Marta and the children, the forest leaning over the sand, Indians and Negroes poling the river on their rafts (though paper was difficult to come by). He was short and bald, with a long, rough beard that had turned completely white from age and salt. His stomach had grown large and round and he wore loose, white linen shirts unbuttoned to his navel, and breeches that revealed his handsome, robust calves. One of Napoleon's generals? No, sir, it was just too much to believe.

But then, sometimes, seen on his horse (first Curado's gift then other, finer animals), seen riding into town or inspecting his plantation, Miguel the Frenchman threw doubt into the minds of those who dismissed the rumours, those who laughed and shook their heads, those who said, '*Senhor*, please, he was never a general in *any* army.' Straight-backed, head high, hips giving precisely with the motion of the horse beneath him, there was an obvious, natural affinity with the animal, an air and grace and authority, even with bare feet in the stirrups, the long beard and big stomach in the saddle. The Frenchman was an impressive sight and for a moment, as he rode by, those who'd doubted would venture their imaginations to a battle-field in Europe (those, at least, who knew that battlefields and Europe existed) and they'd again consider the possibility that had been shaped by rumours, and yes, undoubtedly, there was a fit, a coming together like jigsaw pieces, an unexpected vision. By God, maybe it was true!

And then Miguel would swing down off the horse, and he was just a short old man again and the world returned to recognisable dimensions.

'Marta,' he said, 'my Marta.'

Six brown children, the youngest of them running naked in the yard of their stone house, surrounded by orange, lemon and lime trees, avocado, guava and banana, chickens pecking in the grass, a red parrot perched in a cage hanging from a post in the shade of an awning, squawking out words in French.

'Monsieur! *Assieds-toi!* Mademoiselle! *Assieds-toi!*'

His eldest children married and they all came to live on the estancia that the général built. Grandchildren, dogs, cats twisting around his ankles, the général lay in his hammock or sat in a rocking chair with a large bowl of sweet, milky cocoa and watched his family, contented. He swam at the beaches and rode his horse on the trails. He made love to his beautiful Pataxó wife, outside on the hot nights, on a blanket beneath the cool stars.

He never saw Curado again. Over time, he thought less and less of Bonaparte.

Sometimes he remembered Elisabeth von Hoffmann.

THE CAT

Each stroke diminished the man, stripped him naked, ripped him raw, exposed and hopeless, dropped him into the pit of his greatest agony.

Every man (except Turner) one hundred lashes: an eternity.

Strapped to a triangle of wood made smooth from the pain-rub of others, John Myer couldn't turn his head to see behind.

Every pause between strokes was loaded with the cruel promise of reprieve. Twenty-two down and counting.

'Is it stingin' yet, sweetie?'

The scourger knew his trade and all the tricks. Wet and salt the leather, then let dry in the sun until the knots and the tails are pip hard. Then space the flogging, count slow tens in between. The slower you go, the better you break them.

John Myer heard the twist of the scourger's boot in the dirt, then the grunt and now the strike, a splash of hot knotted lines, stars of fire across his back.

The skin can split as early as the fifth, the flesh tear. They said it depends on the way you're made.

All written down in the book, beside John Myer's name. An ink notch for every stroke, the ink hand neat, meticulous. About an hour, a hundred strokes, give or take.

KRÜGER'S LITTLE FINGER

Not long after Bonaparte's final exile to St Helena, Dr Antoine Girodet sold his property and business interests in Cayenne and returned to live in France.

He settled back in Montpellier with his wife and sister-in-law, in a house on rue Lallemond, not far from the Musée d'Anatomie, to which he'd hoped to bequeath his copious notes, diaries and statistical recordings, as well as hundreds of skulls and skeletons he'd collected during his guillotine experiments. Unfortunately, everything was lost when the long boat taking his possessions out to the ship bound for France sank in a rough sea. Devastated, Girodet never recovered. His life's work, sunk to the murky bottom, and no way to begin again.

By the time he'd sailed back to France, the doctor had entered a black depression. A period of sharp mental and physical decline began. Before the year was ended, his hands were shaking and his head twitched. He could barely recognise his wife and sister-in-law, until he couldn't at all. Every memory fled his mind, one by one, until his head was merely a shell, made only of echoes and distances.

The life he'd lived in Cayenne drifted into dream, and then elsewhere. There were no guillotines, no black skulls rolling into baskets, no blood, no death. There was nothing.

Except, sometimes, like a miracle, there was Josephine. Sometimes he woke with the beautiful mulatto girl before his eyes, wondering who she was and unable to recall, and yet there was the feeling that he must have known her once.

Of course, by the time Girodet had risen from his bed, his mind had fallen limp like a flag again, and the feeling of remembering something faded and everything was forgotten, until possibly the next morning, or the next week, or in a month's time when his mind randomly renewed her again and it was like the first time (who was she?), and the dark-skinned girl was always the same dream and then always forgotten and never to be known.

Some months later, he died. His wife and sister-in-law were present in the room. Moments before passing, Dr Antoine Girodet had shouted, 'His little finger!' and then exhaled his last breath. The two women, hands clasped and praying in the close silence, had jumped out of their skins (the doctor hadn't spoken for days). They could not imagine what he'd meant, nor would they have understood had Girodet been able to explain. How he'd helped Josephine cut off the white man's finger and pare away the flesh, so she could make herself an *obia* from the bone.

THE WIDOW

In Valdivia, her dead husband's family were cold (the youngest sister the coldest) and later, when it was clear that Elisabeth Montoya wished to stay in the city and continue living in her husband's house, they were unforgiving and vindictive. They treated Elisabeth as though she herself had killed their son and brother. Through lawyers and important contacts in the city hierarchy of aristocrats and politicians, they tried to prevent her from claiming anything of Alejandro's estate (even applying for bailiffs to remove her from the house, though this was unsuccessful). They were tenacious and unchristian. They filed lawsuits and spread terrible rumours about her all over the city. They paid for anonymous articles in the newspapers, sowed scandal and innuendo, careful only not to name her directly, though it was clear who their subject was.

They even hired a parade of actresses to knock on the door, claiming to be former lovers, weeping and dressed in black, to ask Elisabeth to respectfully return some item they had given Alejandro as a gift.

If at first she appeared stubborn and determined to the public observing the battle, who could only interpret Elisabeth's refusal to leave the house and abandon her claim as blatant and shameful profiteering (a whore's profiteering), then it was only because the girl was in shock and alone and exhausted by her grief. But the Montoya family's assault was relentless and soon enough Elisabeth did become both stubborn and determined. It was a natural von Hoffmann tendency besides, one she shared with her aunt Margaretha.

She wrote to Ojeda in Caracas, who recommended a young lawyer, Agustin José Larrain. 'He is keen and capable,' Ojeda replied. 'Keep faith, dear Elisabeth!'

It was strange to be in Alejandro's house. Though in a good street and three storeys high, with a small stable in the rear and a beautiful staircase inside, it was modest and warm in feeling, and Elisabeth saw in the simple furnishings and unadorned walls the calm, generous spirit of her husband. There was a courtyard in the centre with a well and there were lemon trees and flowering vines that climbed up the stone and wound through the balcony railings. A hammock there, too, and she often saw Alejandro lying in its tender sling, though his image would not hold for long and faded with the passing days.

It took many months, but the young lawyer successfully defended her claims. Clear of the Montoya family (though they still paid the scandal sheets to print malicious stories about her), Elisabeth began to live as a woman of independent means, beholden to nobody, with many interests and holdings in and around Valdivia, including property, silver and tin mines, and shipping. Soon enough, the dark-haired and moustachioed Valdivian gentlemen, and the tall, discreet, barbered English officers stationed in the city, pursued and wooed Elisabeth Montoya; she was never short of suitors. And there was a moment or two over the years when her emotions intensified and the thought of being loved again was a temptation and a comfort, and she considered their proposals; but no sooner had she indulged the possibility than they were let go.

Love should never draw from the well of loneliness.

HELL'S GATES

Twenty days to get there and barely two hundred sea miles, in their agony they'd prayed the ship crushed upon the rocks. Then five more days anchored in the wave surges and rains, waiting for the pilot to row out and guide them through the heads.

Not named Hell's Gates for nothing, this cruel sandbar with only a narrow channel to course, treacherous tidal waves sweeping left and right.

'The bastards could've hanged us to begin with!'

In the end, only one soul lost, seaman Toby Price, sixteen and born in Penzance, who fell overboard and was sucked under the hull and never came up again.

In Macquarie Harbour (vast as a sea and foamy) they were given government issue on Settlement Island, then taken in a launch to their new home on Small Island. Then made to swim for it in their coarse new clothes (there was no jetty), or given rope if they couldn't, hauled like dead meat through the freezing water.

A guard said to John Myer, 'Get used to being wet.'

Trees were the work, for ship construction, mostly Huon pine (seventy feet high, fifteen around the trunk, impossible to sink or water rot), plus a little acacia, celery-top and myrtle when they found it. Lop the branches and axe the bark, slide them down the hill banks, along perilous narrow paths cut through the forest and lined with smaller logs and a thick carpet of mulch spread around to help the timber move over the boggy ground, though it never worked that well, nothing ever worked that well, they were never so lucky. Then roll the logs into the shallows when they got to the bottom, chain the lengths together, push them out into the water (up to your neck in it) towards the boats, row the pine rafts across the harbour, then loose them, float them over, drag them up the slipways with hooks and handspikes, tons at a time, for the shipwrights to work. Everything, every day, every week, month, year, on a breakfast of nothing much.

Nothing much, so you wouldn't run. Nothing much because the walls of an empty stomach were harder to breach than walls of stone and iron bars. Nothing much because there wasn't much of anything anyway, except rain.

But it was easy to get away, if you were desperate enough, the forest like diving into a deep green sea. Everybody tried, at least once or twice.

John Myer lasted six days the first time, until finally he was going around in circles. Every path forged ate him up and spat him back the way he'd come. Deep rushing rivers cut him off, cliffs loomed, the rain never stopped. Twisted, spiky growth tall as horses reared on him, and distant mountains made him cower in the shadows of their impossible foothills.

He ate a fish raw. He chewed leaves, roots, until he was sick with stomach cramps. They caught him curled up and sweating a fever on a bed of moss by a creek, a small waterfall behind throwing silver mist and glistening the trees.

Sentenced to one hundred lashes and six months' hard labour in a work gang. Sentence remitted (fifty lashes) by Commandant John Cuthbertson.

Cuthbertson had reviewed the prisoner's record and contrived the remittance. Here in this brutal wilderness, at the edge of the world and lacking assets, the legal precedents and conventions were null and void. Reality was enough to shift abstract perspectives. New orders were required and so evolved. Cuthbertson was a drinker, but he knew how to read the swirly script in any given situation. He needed more guards, for Christ's sake. And convict constables when he couldn't get them.

'Bring me Myer,' he said.

The guard brought John Myer to see the commandant after his wounds from the flogging had been treated (soaked rags) and he was able to stand and walk again. Fifty lashes, not so bad: John Myer's back had hardened some time ago.

'Prussian, so I hear,' the commandant said. He was rheumy-eyed, runny-nosed, rough rum on his rancid breath. 'A fine military culture.'

John Myer stood there, swayed a little, his back still on fire, said nothing.

'You've worn a uniform, held a musket,' the commandant said. He could see pain twisting the man's face and hoped his words were registering. 'A professional soldier, and with years of experience. I've a proposition for you, lad.'

BOOK IX

BOOK IX

THE COLONIAL TIMES

February 4th, 1834

*News has reached town this morning that the new schooner,
the* Frederick, *built at Macquarie Harbour, and which had
been expected to arrive in Hobart Town for the last three weeks,
has been piratically seized by the prisoners left at that abandoned settlement, for the purpose of bringing the vessel to this
port. Captain Taw has arrived by the mail this morning from
Launceston, bringing the above intelligence. It appears that
the prisoners took advantage of some of the soldiers being on a
fishing expedition, when they overpowered the remainder, and
took forcible possession of the vessel. The* Frederick *is spoken
of as being a fast sailing vessel, and as the pirates have had
three weeks' start, there is little chance of their capture.*

A DEATH IN THE FAMILY

Aunt Margaretha passed away that year.

On the morning she received the letter from Berlin (it had
taken eight months to reach Valdivia) Elisabeth Montoya went

out to the markets to buy flowers for the house. Her maid Samanta came with a large wicker basket and they filled it with white, red and yellow roses, peonies and lilies and purple bellflowers. The sky was clear and high, the sea was gentle and everything was beautiful and bright. The scent of flowers in the crisp air was intoxicating as they walked between the colourful stalls.

Elisabeth thought of her aunt. She recalled Margaretha now with love, free of any bitterness and the frustrations of her youth; and Elisabeth was sad not because of her aunt's death (we must all die) but because for the first time she understood her aunt as a woman. One who'd lived a long life and been unloved and alone through most of it. And Elisabeth knew that she too had to bear some of her aunt's long life.

She remembered once seeing her aunt in bed, very late in the morning (as per usual), through the door a servant hadn't completely closed behind them. Aunt Margaretha was lying back on her many pillows, head turned to the window, exhausted it seemed to Elisabeth, and grotesquely wigless, her thinning hair revealed, her bare face pale and bloated, cheeks scarred and veined, a wreck of a woman. As her aunt had always been displeased with Elisabeth, had scolded her since she could remember, had never praised but only criticised, she was glad to see the old woman there, defeated and vulnerable.

Elisabeth wished she could have written one more letter to her aunt.

They left the market and went to a bakery for bread and pastries. Then Elisabeth sent Samanta home with the basket of flowers and the food and decided to walk down to the water. She found a bench that looked across the docks and sat down to smoke a cigarette, rolling the tobacco and licking the paper just as Alejandro had taught her all those years ago.

As she lit the cigarette, Elisabeth recognised some ships out on the water that were part of her business interests, unloading cargo and replenishing water barrels. The docks were busy with dozens of luggers coming and going, and there were men leading horse wagons down the piers and carrying sacks on their shoulders and rolling barrels over the smooth flagstones. They wore peasant pants and rope-soled shoes and blue caps. Some of the men looked over at her and smiled. A few were game, tapped fingers to their lips and blew her kisses.

Elisabeth finished her cigarette. She closed her eyes and felt the warmth of the sun on her face. She stayed like that for a long time.

THE *FREDERICK*

When they asked him to join the crew ('Say a word to anyone an' you're fuckin' dead') John Myer didn't hesitate. There was nothing he wouldn't have risked to get away—by this time not even his life, which was only a burden. As the other men pressed him and threatened him, offered the place among them though with coiled reluctance (those stinking, chained, angry men), John Myer had felt the shuddering of the earth beneath his feet, the vibration of it right through his body. He'd arrived at some point that he recognised, that had been waiting for his attention all this time. It was not for him to wonder how or why. All that John Myer knew, intuitively, was there would never be another chance.

Now one of ten desperate men.

Nobody was killed (a few heads were busted) and it was as though the cell keys had been left in the locks. Help yourselves, boys, off you go. And to boot, a nearly finished brig, only a handful of guards (fishing!) and the penal settlement already abandoned except for the convict shipwrights and labourers.

Six weeks later, in the boundless Southern Ocean, they sighted land without a day to spare, their lives in the balance and fading. 'Huzzah!' They cracked the *Frederick*'s hull and sank her, took the longboat into shore. Fixed their stories of shipwrecked sailors and hoped for the best. But never going back, each man swore it in his heart; oh no, never.

'Mutton and rum!' Benjamin Russen said. 'And women to drown in!'

'You'll behave,' James Porter said, eyes on the beach ahead of them. 'We're not in the clear yet.'

John Myer knew it was true. He pulled at the oar, dragged the choppy sea and heaved with gritted teeth. Fatigue heavy through his flesh. Not clear yet, but close.

He was forty-six years old.

SOMETIMES IT HELPS TO OPEN
ALL THE WINDOWS

Samanta was concerned about her mistress. For weeks now the señora rarely left the house. They no longer went together to the flower market or to the bakery for cherry pastries, no longer took walks down to the water in the evening, no longer visited the offices where her businesses were run and the managers and accountants and clerks there greeted her with great respect and manners, pulling out and offering their chairs, even to Samanta. The señora was still a beautiful woman and often courted and always invited to the most fashionable soirées and salons in Valdivia. But she would not attend or be courted any longer. Her fine silk dresses hung sadly in the robe. Samanta believed the señora's malaise had ruined one of the lemon trees in the courtyard. She feared for the health of their well water.

Thankfully (Samanta had been praying to the Virgin) the señora did finally take a walk one day and was gone for most of it. The sun and air would do her great good, Samanta thought. She opened all the windows in the house and all the cupboard doors, and beat the rugs and swept and mopped the floors. She aired the blankets and pillows and she wiped every shelf clean of dust and she chose the brightest table-cloths and cushions for the house. And as she did, Samanta softly repeated the Indian chants her mother had taught her when she was a child, the ones she could only ever whisper in case her father heard them sung, for which crime mother and daughter would both be beaten. The chants were ancient, in the language of her mother's people from the mountains (which Samanta could not otherwise speak or understand), and they dispelled bad spirits and called on the good. She'd always felt the truth of them and was certain the Virgin understood, too. It was never a simple thing, to air a dark home.

Her mother would say, 'An open heart has no secret compartments.'

Samanta lit smudge sticks and chanted the prayers and brushed the smoke over every wall, drawing loops and sweeping arcs, concentrating on the corners that never received sunlight (where the bad spirits cowered). She went to all three floors and through every room, out onto the balconies too, and even up into the attic with its terrible spiders' webs. She could feel her good work giving breath back to the sad house.

When the señora returned, Samanta heard the front door slam, the iron knocker sounding twice. Then along the hall the floorboards creaked with pain and the small vases and glass bowls on the shelves and side tables rattled and shook with the señora's firm striding. A small picture frame slid flat. Samanta came out from the kitchen to see, but her mistress was already on the stairs.

'Señora?' she said.

'You can go home, Samanta.'

'Are you not feeling well?'

Elisabeth paused on the landing, looked down at the girl

but said nothing. She looked right through her and Samanta felt herself shiver.

'I can fix some tea, Señora,' she said. 'Special herbs I have from the mountains, they will help if you are unwell . . .'

'Please, Samanta.' Elisabeth held up her hand. 'Obey me.'

'Yes, Señora.'

Samanta stayed, of course, but was too scared to ascend the stairs and listen at the bedroom door in case the señora heard her coming. She waited in the kitchen. She made the herbal tea and prayed to the Virgin. Samanta knew she couldn't stay all night, but was torn and in two minds. The señora would be very displeased if she discovered her there in the kitchen, but she felt that she should wait, in case she was needed, in case the señora called for her.

Samanta waited but heard nothing. What could the señora be doing? Samanta waited for as long as she could, but when the dark came, the silence seemed to thicken in her ears. She was afraid. Eventually, like a thief, Samanta crept out of the house and hurried home.

The next morning when she returned, the señora gave her money and sent her away to spend time with her family in Los Lagos.

NEW LIFE

He'd taken back his true name and found work unloading ships. He rented a small room in a faded blue hotel, full of scarred, tail-less cats over in the poorer part of town, where the lanes smelled of stale urine and the nights were loud with singing and fighting. He'd bought a book from a street stall and read from it every evening (it was Goethe, in Spanish, he had to read slowly). There was a cantina not far away, where every day Johannes Meyer ate grilled fish and drank sweet white wine the colour of straw.

He took his time with everything, settled into a calm that savoured every moment. He walked unhurriedly, ate slowly, worked hard, slept deeply, read and let his imagination roam. One of the cats adopted him. The hours were long and kind and lingered like welcome guests.

He believed them, these hours, or wanted to, but in truth he remained suspicious of the contentment they seemed to bestow. It lessened over time, this suspicion, but never truly faded. He wondered if it ever would (it wouldn't). His contentment had a cautious air.

He looked over his shoulder from time to time. He approached corners with vague trepidation.

Johannes Meyer was working at the dock one day and he saw her first.

He slid the sack down from his shoulder and brushed the dust from his arm. She was walking towards him with an umbrella against the sun. There was a man with her, short and fat and overdressed, a watch chain bright between his vest pockets, wiping his forehead with a white handkerchief and pointing out into the harbour, showing her the ships. They came closer, walking down the storehouse side of the dock, where the sun blazed hottest against the stone facades. Then they paused for a moment as the man lit the woman's cigarette. When she lifted her head, she was looking directly at Johannes.

They stood like that only metres apart, eyes on each other, each remembering and yet thinking that it couldn't be.

DAYS CAN GO EITHER WAY

She'd sent Samanta away and had been thinking of it for days, recalling the boy at the docks (he wasn't a boy anymore!). Deeply regretting that she hadn't approached and spoken to him. Elisabeth Montoya felt an unaccountable sense of loss.

Her true impulse had been to go over and greet him (embrace him!) but she didn't move, just looked, in a kind of shock. Because he wasn't an old friend, he wasn't anybody at all, just a face from a long time ago, and it was this thought that had percolated among a rush of others and held her there, motionless. And then somebody had yelled, further down the dock, and she'd watched him turn to the voice and then bend down to pick up the sack at his feet. She'd watched him shoulder it, bounce it into position, and then turn to look at her again. And then Señor Bonas (who hadn't stopped talking the whole time) had taken her by the arm and they'd moved on. He was showing her the new dock warehouse that had been purchased.

She wasn't listening to him. She only felt the man's eyes following her. With every step away, she'd thought to stop and turn around, but she didn't.

Elisabeth Montoya walked away with Señor Bonas. With every excruciating step, she hoped to hear him call out, call out after her.

Please, she'd thought. Hoped. Please call out to me.

A LETTER FROM CHILE

(From Consul General Walpole, Santiago de Chile, to Lieutenant Governor George Arthur, Hobart Town, Van Diemen's Land)

May 25th, 1834

Sir: I have the Honour to transmit to you the Translation of a Paragraph contained in the Araucano, *a Paper published here under the Authority of this Government & which was Communicated to me by the Secretary of State for Foreign Affairs.*

By this Paper you will perceive that Ten Individuals whose names are specified in a List also enclosed, presented themselves on the 9th of March last at Valdivia in this Republic stating themselves to have been shipwrecked on the coast of Chile—that the truth of this Account appearing to be liable to doubt, a further Examination into the Circumstances was entered into, the result of which was a declaration of their having absconded from a Port in Van Diemen's Land, thereby withdrawing themselves from the Performance of the Sentence to which they had been sentenced with the Addition of the Committal of an Act which it would seem can only be characterized by the Term of Piracy.

The Circumstances as stated by them appear so contradictory in many Parts and indeed the Confession of the serious Crimes which they profess to have Committed renders their History so improbable that it is scarce possible to attach credit to it.

LIEUTENANT GOVERNOR ARTHUR'S MINUTE UPON RECEIVING THE LETTER

October 31st, 1834

Prepare an answer setting forth all the particulars of the case, with the offences for wh. these Convicts were transported, & adding, of course, that their last act was one of piracy & express my anxious desire that they may be sent back to this Colony & add that as soon as a Vessel of War arrives I shall request the Officer in command of Her to proceed to Valparaiso. Let me see your letter as soon as it is prepared—one copy may be sent to Sydney, another to Rio by the earliest oppty.

BOOK X

HIGH IN THE GREAT WESTERN
TIERS, THREE RIDERS

They stood their horses inside a stand of snow gums. They could see the timber hut just ahead, sheltered in the lee of a small rise that curved out across the plain to the north-west. No smoke in the chimney pipe. The wind had picked up and it was starting to rain, and there were fat snowflakes whipping around in it, too. The trees were sleet wet from the night before, and the trunks gleamed blue-grey and gold, pink where the bark had peeled away.

It was 6 March 1915.

Gabriel Tait shifted in the saddle. It had been a hard slog through densely wooded valleys and up steep mountain banks, and the horse didn't like him. The feeling was mutual. At one point the crazy animal had bolted along a ridge for no reason anybody could give him, a sheer drop to certain death only inches from its sparking shoes. He'd climbed off when it finally stopped, cursing the beast.

'You ain't much of a rider,' Wilson O'Farrell had said.

'He's all right,' his brother Joseph said. He smiled at Gabriel Tait. 'Don't worry, mate. Nearly there.'

He'd had a mind to turn back for Deloraine, be done with it, but they'd come past the halfway by then. The O'Farrell brothers had charged five pounds to bring him up and the paper would want something for the expense.

They sat their horses and waited inside the snow gums, collars up, hats low, watching the hut. Nothing else around for miles. Wind, rain, snow.

THE STORY

'Nobody's a hundred and twenty-six years old,' Gabriel Tait said.

He was twenty-one and there were two or three close friends and his parents in Invermay, and a younger sister as well. And there was a fiancée and there was that he worked for the Launceston *Examiner*. The two or three close friends had already joined up and the fiancée had been telling everybody how Gabriel was joining up, too.

Gabriel Tait's subeditor said, 'Well, that's what they say, one twenty-six. It isn't totally *impossible*, right?'

'Yes it is.'

'Anyway, look, it doesn't matter, I mean, he could be a hundred an' nine or something, you know? People always exaggerate.' Lance Landstrom could tell the boy was reluctant, but he thought there was some talent there needed pushing.

'Like I said, it doesn't matter. He's bloody old, full stop. Just make something of it.'

'Like what?'

'Jesus, come on, Tait. People love this kind of thing,' Landstrom said. 'Or you'd rather stick to shipping news and death notices?' He went back to the typescript on his desk.

On the way home, Gabriel Tait had a few beers in different pubs, asked around. His fiancée was expecting him at seven-thirty, dinner with the future in-laws and some of their family friends, maybe an old aunt up from Hobart. His fiancée had fought hard to bring her parents around to the engagement and the dinner was important. Tait glanced at his watch. Bought a few more rounds.

Nobody had heard of the one hundred-and-twenty-six-year-old man who lived somewhere up in the Great Western Tiers.

'Who? John Myer?' they said. 'Nah.'

A quarter to eight now, at a workers' pub in Mowbray, doors locked. Every second man in uniform. The barman said, 'Sure, I've heard of him. The old Kraut who lives up on the Tiers.'

'Really?'

'Yeah. My poppy knew him. Used to stay over sometimes when he was out trapping. All the old guys did.'

Tait leaned a little over the bar. 'Is he still alive?'

The barman laughed. 'Yeah, and he's about a hundred and fifty years old mate, last I heard.'

'Two 'undred!' said a drunk next to them, laughing into his beer.

At the Langridge's, Evie opened the door. 'You're late!'
'Sorry,' Tait said. 'It's work. I'm on a story.'

FIREWOOD

The clouds rolled in and the snowflakes thickened. Gabriel Tait had never seen such volumes of whiteness in his life, falling silently from the sky, tiny feathers of snow, covering everything. It was beautiful.

He looked over at the O'Farrell brothers and they were watching the snow, too.

'When was the last time you ever saw him up here?' Gabriel Tait said.

The older brother, Wilson, squinted up into the sky and patted his horse on the neck. He was tall and rangy, with bluestone eyes in a dark, sooty face. He ignored the question and nudged his horse on.

'Oh, been a while,' said Joseph O'Farrell, who was nothing like his brother. He was shorter, had a cottage pie body, and a natural, easy warmth. He clicked his tongue, gave on the reins and followed. 'Years,' he said over his shoulder to Tait.

They rode over to the hut. Rough planks of lichen-patched wood, a shingle roof, animal skins nailed over a window space to the right of the door, the bottom corner loose and flapping. They skirted around to the right. In the rear there was a small, low awning attached to the hut, walled off on two sides with more timber planks.

They put the horses in and the brothers slipped off the bridles and unsaddled them, then Joseph hooked on their nosebags for a chew. They picked up a rail (a narrow tree trunk, axe-trimmed) and slotted it into a couple of brackets either side of the opening. The wind had eased off but the snow kept falling.

'Better be some firewood,' Wilson O'Farrell said.

'We'll have a look,' Joseph said.

His brother walked back around to the front of the hut, carrying a rifle and the sack that had hung from his pommel.

Joseph tapped Tait on the shoulder. 'Come on, give us a hand.'

There was a woodpile a little way from the hut.

'It's all wet,' Tait said, feeling colder just looking at it.

'Choice cuts underneath.'

They picked up an armful of wood each, made their way back to the hut.

'He hasn't been here for a long time,' Tait said.

'Doesn't look like it,' Joseph O'Farrell said. 'But that doesn't mean he's not around.'

Tait looked at him, confused. He couldn't read the tone. The brothers had spoken to him like that the whole way, smiling underneath every word, nothing ever certain about what they were saying.

Joseph O'Farrell saw the annoyed look on Tait's face and stopped. 'You wanted to see where he lived, right? Well, this is it.' He opened a gloved palm to the falling snow. 'And looks like we're staying the bloody night now, too.'

They took the firewood into the hut.

LOVE IS SACRIFICE

At school, everybody thought Evangeline Langridge had airs and graces.

'Just because her father owns a newspaper,' they said. 'Who cares?'

She was seventeen, serious like her father, broad like her mother, and though her features didn't add up to any remarkable beauty, taken separately there was nothing to fault: large brown eyes, soft pink cheeks, tawny hair that fell long down her back when it wasn't plaited and pinned up. It was glimpsing her hair one day (through a door left ajar in the hallway, her back to him, hair loose and wavy and cascading all the way to her waist), which had thrilled Gabriel Tait the first time. He hadn't been long at the paper, had come to deliver something to the boss. Soon they went to dinner every Thursday and soon after that they went riding together on Saturdays.

Matters progressed (though her hair remained pinned) until Evie asked Tait to propose to her. He'd frowned, surprised, and then she'd laughed; but Evie meant it, and eventually Tait did as she wished, though the moments leading to his asking and those that came after were a blur to him now.

He'd done it, and Tait supposed he was happy about it, but wasn't exactly sure why. He could hardly tell people it was because of her hair. And then (due to Evie's tenacity) there'd been the announcement and it didn't really matter anymore.

His mother and father were very happy. His sister hated Evangeline Langridge.

'Everybody's waiting,' Evie said to her fiancé.

Tait took off his coat, heavy with the smell of tobacco and beer, hung it on the rack by the door. He was suddenly oppressed by the thought of the Langridges' dining room, just down the hall and to the right. The dark wood and crystal light and fine bone china, the expensive candles that made it smell like a church. Mr and Mrs there, and the old aunt from Hobart, and whichever guests to fill out the enormous table and agree with Mr Langridge's unimpeachable opinions on infinite subjects. And Evie, always answering for Tait, as though nervous he might say something wrong and embarrass everyone.

'Who's here?' Tait said, following Evie down the hall.

She didn't say, but hurried along to the dining room door, opened it, smiled broadly and said, 'Finally!' as she walked in, as though she'd had to go out and physically look for her fiancé in the streets.

'Gabriel, where have you been?' Mrs Langridge said.

'Working, Mother, where else?' Evie said. 'Working hard.'

'My apologies, Mrs Langridge,' Tait said and sat down. He looked around the table. The beer was in his heartbeat and he could taste nicotine on his lips and the room stretched out into his peripheral vision and for sure it had been a folly to come. Now endure.

Mr Langridge nodded silently at him.

'You remember Mr and Mrs Ainsley, Gabriel,' Evie said.

'Yes, of course.'

'Mr Ainsley was just telling us about their two boys,' Mr Langridge said. He was a tall, angular man with, it seemed, only one stern expression ever available to his face. 'George and Frank have joined up.' He looked over at the door and motioned for the butler to begin serving.

'Light horse,' Mr Ainsley said.

'Handsome lads,' Mr Langridge said. 'We'll have them in the paper, Wednesday edition.' He paused. 'Maybe you could give it a few words, Gabriel.'

'Of course, Mr Langridge.'

'Good man.'

Mrs Ainsley began to sob.

'Miriam!' her husband said.

Evie went over to the woman, put an arm around her shoulder. 'It's all right, Mrs Ainsley,' she said and rubbed her arm. 'It's all right.'

'No need to fret, Miriam,' Mrs Langridge said. 'It will all turn out just fine.'

Mrs Ainsley smiled sadly, regained control. 'I'm sorry.' She wanted to say they were only boys, but she'd seen the hard look on her husband's face. 'Silly me!'

'They're a credit to you,' Mr Langridge said, 'and the pride of Tasmania.' He raised his glass.

Everybody followed suit. Tait reached across for the glass that had been poured for him and knocked it over, spilling wine across the white tablecloth.

'Bloody hell,' Mr Langridge said.

OFFICIAL DOCUMENTS

Before Gabriel Tait left for the Tiers with the O'Farrells, the subeditor Lance Landstrom had said, 'You might want to read some of the stuff in the records. Get a little background on the guy. He was a convict, you know.'

'Sure.'

'Take a few days,' Landstrom said. 'You'll have to go down to Hobart.'

'The paper's paying, right?'

'Ask your future father-in-law.'

Tait caught a morning train to Hobart. The capital was grey and overcast, just like the last time he'd seen it. Evie had wanted to come along but her parents wouldn't hear of it. Tait was relieved, glad to get out of town for a while on his own.

The clerk at the Chief Secretary's Department led Gabriel Tait down into a basement. It was somewhere under Franklin

Square, completely dark, cold, smelled musty and damp. The clerk flicked a switch and something crackled; a single electric globe at the end of a thick black wire in the ceiling lit up, threw weak yellow light. There were open-backed timber shelves against the sandstone walls and dissecting the space in rows, stacked with boxes and huge ledgers, their leather bindings rotted and peeling from the boards. There were more documents piled up on the floor in lopsided towers, all along and at the ends of each row.

'Convict records?' Tait said.

'No idea, mate,' the clerk said. 'In here somewhere.' He pointed to a small table and chair. 'You can use that. We close at four.' The clerk headed back up the stairs.

Tait stood for a moment, looking at the shelves, the boxes, ledgers and files. The subterranean quiet had already leeched the space of their voices from only seconds before. The stillness was tomb-like. Only the faint buzzing of electric light hooked his ear, the sole link to the surface.

He took off his hat, tossed it onto the table. He lit a cigarette and went over to the nearest shelf. He looked for some kind of label designation, cataloguing numbers and dates, but there was nothing. He flipped open one of the ledgers. A document slipped to the floor.

There were thousands of documents, maybe tens of thousands. Tait looked for John Myer among them. He couldn't find him that first day. He couldn't find him on the second or the third or the fourth day either.

'How's it going down there?' the clerk said.

'Great,' Tait said.

RUMOURS

'So, I hear you're getting married.'

It was the first thing Wilson O'Farrell had said in at least an hour.

'Who told you I was getting married?' Tait said.

'Nobody,' Wilson O'Farrell said. 'Just heard the whisper.'

The fire was going and outside it was already dark and the snow was still falling in long, heavy drifts. They'd discovered a possum in the flue before and the hut was still reeking of piss and adrenaline, the animal hissing and scratching after Wilson had wrapped his arm in rags and reached up into the pipe, trying to grab it. Then he'd attempted to smoke it out, but the fire wouldn't pull cleanly to flame ('We're going to freeze to death 'cause of this bloody thing') and then finally he'd had to climb up onto the roof with his rifle and shoot the possum down the chimney.

Tait stared at Wilson. Joseph smiled and patted him on the shoulder. 'Second cousin, mate,' he said. 'Mother's side.'

'Excuse me?'

'Evie Langridge. We're related. We used to play together when we were kids.'

Jesus, thought Gabriel Tait.

'Evie's great,' Joseph said. 'Haven't seen her in a while though.'

'She's moved up in the world,' Wilson O'Farrell said, poking at the fire. 'No more playing with little Joe.' He turned to his brother. 'Anything to drink?'

Joseph stood up. 'I'll have a look.'

The hut was cobwebbed and there were mouse droppings over the floor and dust over everything, but it was dry and well sealed, the wind only reaching in under the door as it gusted now and then, rattling the latch, or when it whinnied through the edges of the animal skin over the window. There was a small table, two chairs and a bench along the left-side wall, stacked timber boxes and a slatted bed frame in the corner (with a straw mattress of sewn hessian sacks) and an improvised shelf with wooden crates slotted in like drawers. Rusted nails in the exposed studwork, one or two with the withered twig remains of some plant, a thin chain on another, a small painting (blue water bay) hanging by the bed. Cutlery, a stack of tins with no labels, a hatchet, jug and bowl on a stand below a mirror the size of a postcard. Tait had noticed a few books on a shelf too, but hadn't gone to look yet.

Joseph O'Farrell said, 'Here we go,' and held up a bottle of whisky.

'Good work, brother.'

'They say he's German,' Tait said.

'Prussian,' Wilson said.

'Long way to come.'

'True for everybody here, ain't it?'

Joseph found cups and poured.

'How'd you meet him?' Tait asked.

'Our old man used to send us up with supplies,' Joseph said. 'John let us stay the night sometimes, depending on the weather or how late we got in.'

'What was he doing up here?'

Wilson smiled. 'Hunting tigers.'

'Seriously?'

'Why not?'

Gabriel Tait looked into his cup. He didn't believe it; but, then, he wasn't sure what to believe about John Myer. He said, 'So did he really crack a hundred? Or the one twenty-six, like they say?'

'I reckon he got the century for sure,' Joseph said. 'At least.'

'And then some,' his brother said.

'Yeah, you're right.'

Tait said, 'Do you know his age for a fact?'

'Knew it with me own eyes,' Wilson said. 'Standing next to the man.'

'That doesn't tell me when he was born.'

'Reckon he was though.'

Tait sipped his drink. 'There's a story then.'

'Well,' Wilson said and swept his arm around the hut, 'it's all here, matey. You only paid us to get you up.'

They sipped their whiskies.

'He was married,' Tait said. He'd found the names in a marriage register in the archives in Hobart.

'Yeah?' Wilson said. 'Didn't know. He might have been.'

'John was a handsome chap,' Joseph said. 'That's true.'

DARCEY'S LUCKY WEDDING RINGS

Every morning in Hobart, Gabriel Tait waited for the Chief Secretary's Department to open its doors. Because he couldn't sleep, he was always up early and nothing was open and hardly anybody was about.

He walked around town and paused under the shop awnings. He wanted to buy something for Evie before he left, though he hadn't seen anything yet. He looked into the windows but, really, it was only absently.

All week, the wind was icy down off Mount Wellington.

Tait was staying at the Criterion Hotel in Liverpool Street. They did a good lunch and the room had electricity and a bath. In the evenings after dinner, he read the newspapers, front to back. He read the headline stories (*Gallant British Troops*) and he read the advertisements, too (*Richard Darcey. Ring Specialist. You Find the Girl, I'll Find the Ring. 84 Liverpool Street. PRICES TO SUIT ALL POCKETS*). After that, Tait usually went to bed and tried to read a book.

Evie had lent him *Wuthering Heights*, but he just couldn't get a bite on it.

CHILE

Wilson O'Farrell made strong black tea and heaped half-a-dozen teaspoons of sugar into the pot. Joseph poured a good splash of whisky into their cups and passed around a tin of shortbreads he'd brought along.

'Mum makes the best,' he said. He put them down on the floor between them. 'Help yourself.'

'Just go easy,' Wilson said, looking at Tait. 'There's three of us.'

They sat in front of the fire and watched the flames while the snow gums outside heaved in the gusts of wind and snow. Around them, the timber hut strained and creaked into its joists. The leaves that had blown into the corners sometimes flipped over in the draught. Wilson had his wet boots and socks off now, resting his feet on a crate.

'They'll catch fire in a minute,' Joseph said.

'Good. Can barely feel me toes.'

'Kill the stench at least.'

Wilson reached down for another biscuit.

'What about cards?' Joseph said.

'Nah,' his brother said. 'I hate fucking cards.'

'That's 'cause you can't play.' Joseph looked at Tait. 'You?'

Tait shook his head.

'Then I'll have to play myself.'

Wilson O'Farrell laughed. 'You'll have to what? Play with yourself?'

'Yeah, that's exactly what I said.'

'You heard it, Tait!'

Joseph ignored his brother, dragged across a box and spread his legs to either side. He began shuffling a deck of cards.

'So did he ever tell you how he escaped to Chile?' Tait said.

'Never told us much about anything, really.'

'All that way and then they brought him back again.' Four of them were caught, John Myer last of all, down at the Valdivia docks. The *North Star* to England and then the *Sarah* back to Van Diemen's Land. Another trial in 1837 and then serving out his sentence at Port Arthur. Married in 1849. Tait sipped his whisky-laced tea. 'Imagine that.' He'd found it all in the records. A few words in ink, this hut; all that remained of a man.

'Not me, mate,' Wilson said. 'No bloody way.'

His brother looked up from his cards. 'No way what?'

'Sailing the high seas.'

Joseph laughed. 'You will be soon, but. You'll be sailing your arse off.'

'That's different.'

'How?'

'Well, it's a big bloody iron boat with no sails and they know where they're going an' I just have to sit there, right?' Wilson O'Farrell grabbed his foot, rubbed it and wiggled his long, bony toes. The muster for the front was the day after next.

'Still the same high seas,' his brother said, flipping cards.

HANDCUFFS AND LEG IRONS

They finished the tea and the whisky, too. The fire was blazing. Joseph O'Farrell found a second bottle.

'Show him the cuffs,' Wilson said.

'Want to see them?'

'Sure,' Tait said.

Joseph went to the shelves stacked with crates and pulled one out and put it on the floor. 'The very ones they clamped on the poor bastard.'

Tait sat up now and moved to the edge of his chair. He watched Joseph take a few things out of the crate and then reach deep into it, his hand rummaging until there was the sound of metal scraping on the thin wood. He pulled his arm out and held up a rusty set of handcuffs.

'Nasty things,' Joseph said. 'The English type with the ratchet arms, makes them really tight.' He handed them to Tait.

'Try 'em on,' Wilson said.

'No thanks.'

'Don't you want to know what it was like?' Wilson checked his socks in front of the fire, turned them over.

Tait stared down at the cuffs in his hands, thinking of John Myer. Thinking, *this lonely hut.*

'We used to play bushrangers with them,' Joseph said. 'The thing you don't think of is how hard it is to run with your hands cuffed behind your back.'

'You'd fall over all the time,' Wilson said.

'Wils was always the law; I had to try and escape,' Joseph said. He pointed at the cuffs. 'One time the ratchet arms got stuck and we couldn't get 'em off. Had to wear the bloody things for a day and a bit.'

Wilson laughed. 'I had to pull his trousers down so he could take a leak.'

'And give me something to eat.'

'Bread and water.'

'And the time you put the leg irons on me.'

'Barefoot, like they used to do.'

'Took the skin right off my ankles.'

'Then I had to bash the things with a hammer to slip the rivets.'

'Big toe went black and blue.'

'Ha!'

'Yeah,' Joseph said. 'Swelled up so I couldn't walk. Real funny.'

'Go on,' Wilson said to Tait. 'Try 'em on. You can use it in your story.'

'GREENSLEEVES'

Gabriel Tait knew that Evie would love the music box. It had cost him a week's wages. She'd love it, and then most probably she'd hate it.

On the train back to Launceston he stared out the window and watched the empty, damp yellow paddocks sweep by, crows lifting out of the scrawled gumtrees in the distance, the sky streaked with thin clouds.

Had John Myer come this way? Tait tried to imagine the man, head down and trudging the bristled bush, searching for the place where he might no longer be called to account for his existence.

WAITING

Gabriel Tait said, 'You signed up?'

Wilson nodded, rolling a cigarette, tongue poking out the corner of his mouth.

Joseph had his eyes closed. 'Yairp.'

The second bottle of whisky had about a third left. They passed it around and swigged straight from the neck. The hut glowed with amber light, warm like a promise; but soon the whisky would be drunk and the fire would burn down and then the light (this light) would be gone.

Gabriel Tait wanted to tell them about John Myer's wife. That she was most likely his great-grandmother, Mary Myer, née Richardson, who died in childbirth. He believed it, knew it for sure when he saw the record. Mary Myer, whom the family never mentioned, because she'd married a convict and then died, her child taken away and raised by a sister. Mary Myer, gone to all but saved in the marriage register with pen and ink. And where was the child? Where had this other line run?

'Go on, then,' Gabriel Tait said and suddenly stood up.

He wobbled a little on his feet and put his hands behind his back. 'Arrest me.'

Joseph smiled, reached for the handcuffs on the floor and got to his feet.

'Make sure they're tight,' Wilson said.

'Yep.'

'Maybe we should put the leg irons on, too.'

'Yeah!'

Everybody awake. Second wind.

'Do it,' Gabriel Tait said.

THERE'S A WAR ON

The music box and the letter arrived from Hobart and Mrs Langridge gave it to her daughter and Evie saw the handwriting and knew straight off that it was from Gabriel.

'Why is he writing to you?' Mrs Langridge said. Instantly, she'd a bad feeling and she didn't like this letter, not at all. 'He's supposed to be back in a few days.'

Evie smiled. 'Mother! Have you never heard of romance?' She took the letter to her room to read in private.

Of course, her mother's instincts were right. The music box was too beautiful, the letter in the envelope was too thick: its effects were immediate.

When Jack Langridge came home, his daughter was weeping in her room. The door was locked and his wife was standing outside it, wringing her hands and pleading with their daughter.

'Evie, open the door! My love, please, open the door!'

Langridge stomped down the dark hallway. Never a moment's peace from these women. 'What in God's name?'

'It's that Tait boy!' his wife said. 'He's written her a letter!'

Evie wailed from behind the door. 'No! Shut up!'

'A letter?'

Mrs Langridge glared at her husband. She'd never defied him or argued with him or pressed a point in all of their twenty years of marriage; but he was an oaf, had always been an oaf. 'Do you need it spelled out? He's broken their engagement!'

'Be calm, woman,' Langridge said, though he was shocked at the way she'd looked at him. He rapped on Evie's door with hard knuckles. 'And best be calm in there, too.'

'Oh, go away, Daddy! I hate you!'

'Fine.'

He did just that. Went to his study, poured a Scotch. His daughter's sobbing still reached him, muffled by the walls between them.

There's a war on, for Christ's sake.

Jack Langridge downed the Scotch and poured another.

HANGOVERS

It had stopped snowing by the morning. The sky was pale and windswept, the light sharp off the bright snow and the O'Farrell brothers squinted out across the white ground. It'd melt by the afternoon.

'We can't hang about,' Wilson said. 'We'll miss the muster.'

'I know.'

'He'll be no good for the ride.'

They'd already made a breakfast of tea sweetened with condensed milk, and Joseph had made damper and then Wilson had fried some bacon with a knob of lard, the brothers wiping up the pan with their crusts. Gabriel Tait didn't stir the whole time, not even with the smell of frying bacon, which had hooked the brother's hangovers and made them salivate.

'I'll get the horses ready,' Wilson said.

'You'd better saddle his, too. He'll need it later.'

Joseph went back into the hut. He tried Tait again, shaking him firmly by the shoulder, but the boy was deeply, drunkenly asleep. The cuffs were still hanging from one of his wrists (the ratchet arm had caught again) but they'd at least managed to get the leg irons off. Joseph pulled Tait's blanket up to his chin and added a log to the fire, then collected their things and rolled their swags and picked up his brother's rifle and put everything outside. He filled a jug with snow and put it on the floor beside Tait. There was some tea left in the pot, some damper and bacon, too.

'See you later, mate.'

Outside, Wilson waited with the horses.

'Reckon he'll be right?' Joseph said.

'Yeah,' Wilson said. 'Just the one track to town. Not that hard to follow.'

BOOK XI

BOOK XI

STENDHAL

After the first barrage, the boy beside Gabriel Tait was instantly killed, hit by shrapnel in the neck and chest. His eyes were still open, unbelieving.

Tait's ears were ringing. The world was one enormous crazy high note, a clutch of piano keys struck by a giant's fist. He couldn't hear the German cannons and machine guns, still thumping shells and bullets into the ground, into sandbags, into men. IIe could only see the horror of his surrounds, inside the high-pitched whine in his head.

But what Gabriel Tait knew, what passed through his mind in the last moments of his life, was that the dead boy beside him had a silver ring under his tongue. And in his blood-soaked breast pocket there was a letter from his sister.

She'd sent the silver ring folded inside a passage from Stendhal. It was from *Les Privilèges*. The boy's older sister had been studying in Paris when the war began. She loved Stendhal and she loved her brother. She'd translated the passage for him. It was an offering to the gods, a prayer, a hymn, a wish that would never fail to resist death. A guarantee: enshrined, worded, printed, unimpeachable. She loved her brother very much.

Article 8: Whenever the privileged person shall carry, for two minutes, on his person or wear on his finger, a ring that he has briefly put in his mouth, he will remain invulnerable for whatever duration he determines. Ten times a year, he shall enjoy the sharp eyesight of an eagle and will be able to run a distance of five leagues within an hour.

She'd sent the ring and the letter to her brother, and the boy had shown it all to Gabriel Tait just now, read the letter out and popped the ring under his tongue, laughing.

And then the shelling began.

It was 19 July 1916.